The Outlaws
of Mesquite

Bantam Books by Louis L'Amour
Ask your bookseller for the books you have missed

SHORT STORY COLLECTIONS

BOWDRIE
BOWDRIE'S LAW
BUCKSKIN RUN
DUTCHMAN'S FLAT
THE HILLS OF HOMICIDE
LAW OF THE DESERT BORN
LONG RIDE HOME
LONIGAN
NIGHT OVER THE
  SOLOMONS
THE RIDER OF THE RUBY
  HILLS
RIDING FOR THE BRAND
THE STRONG SHALL LIVE
THE TRAIL TO CRAZY MAN
WAR PARTY
WEST FROM SINGAPORE
YONDERING

SACKETT TITLES

SACKETT'S LAND
TO THE FAR BLUE
  MOUNTAINS
THE WARRIOR'S PATH
JUBAL SACKETT
RIDE THE RIVER
THE DAYBREAKERS
SACKETT
LANDO
MOJAVE CROSSING
MUSTANG MAN
THE LONELY MEN
GALLOWAY
TREASURE MOUNTAIN
LONELY ON THE MOUNTAIN
RIDE THE DARK TRAIL
THE SACKETT BRAND
THE SKY-LINERS

NONFICTION

FRONTIER
EDUCATION OF A
  WANDERING MAN
THE SACKETT COMPANION:
  A Personal Guide to the
  Sackett Novels
A TRAIL OF MEMORIES:
  The Quotations of
  Louis L'Amour, compiled by
  Angelique L'Amour

THE OUTLAWS OF MESQUITE

———————

Frontier Stories by
Louis L'Amour

BANTAM BOOKS
NEW YORK · TORONTO · LONDON · SYDNEY · AUCKLAND
A Bantam Large Print Edition

THE OUTLAWS OF MESQUITE

A Bantam Book / June 1990
Bantam Large Print Edition / July 1990

ISBN 0-385-41542-7

Published simultaneously in the United States and Canada

Bantam Books are published by Bantam Books, a division of Bantam
Doubleday Dell Publishing Group, Inc. Its trademark, consisting of the
words "Bantam Books" and the portrayal of a rooster, is Registered in U.S.
Patent and Trademark Office and in other countries. Marca Registrada.
Bantam Books, 666 Fifth Avenue, New York, New York 10103.

PRINTED IN THE UNITED STATES OF AMERICA

BVG   0 9 8 7 6 5 4 3 2 1

This Large Print Book carries the
seal of approval of N.A.V.H.

Editor's Note

The Author's Notes preceding each of the stories you are about to read are adapted from recording sessions conducted with Louis L'Amour for his Introductions to the audio dramatizations of his short stories, available from Bantam Audio Publishing on cassette tapes.

Contents

The Outlaws
of Mesquite

Author's Note

The Mesquite I wrote about in this story is a rustler town, a holdup man's town, and it's quite unlike most towns in the West.

In more traditional towns, there were generally two sections. There was the part where the saloons and the red-light district were, what we still refer to today as the wrong side of the tracks, where most of the rough stuff like gunfights went on. On the other side there were churches and schools and citizens carrying on their lives the way normal people would.

Sometimes all the law-abiding people knew about the gunfights across the way was the sound of gunfire. They didn't know who was shooting whom until they heard about it later.

Milt Cogar was at the corral catching the paint when Thacker walked down from the store. "You'd better get out of this town, boy. They are fixin' to make trouble for you."

Milt turned around and looked at the big, clumsy man, his shirt stuffed into his trousers and held there by a rope belt. Thacker never seemed to have a full beard and always seemed to need a shave. His watery blue eyes looked vague. He rolled his quid in his jaws and spat.

"It's what I'm tellin' you, son. You done me a favor or two."

"Why should they be after me?" Cogar demanded. He was a lean young man with a dark, leatherlike face. His eyes were almost black, and keen.

"Spencer wants your horses. You know that. He sets a sight of store by good horseflesh, and he's had a thorn in his side ever since you rode into the valley. Anyway, you're a stranger, and this country don't cotton to strangers."

Milt Cogar hitched his gun belts and stared at Thacker. "Thanks. I'll not forget it. But betwixt the two of us, this country has reason to be afraid of strangers."

Thacker's eyes shifted uneasily. "Don't you be sayin' that aloud. Not around here. And don't you tell nobody what I said."

Thacker drifted off down toward his shack, and Milt Cogar stood there, uncertainly. He was not ready to drift, nor did he like being pushed, but he had sensed the undercurrent of feeling against him.

Mesquite was a rustler town. It was a holdup man's town, and he was a wild horse wrangler and a drifter. He threw the saddle on the paint and cinched it down. All the while he was thinking of Jennie Lewis, for she was the reason he had stayed on at Mesquite.

Milt Cogar was no trouble-hunting man. He knew that of himself and he told that to himself once more. In nearly thirty years of drifting, he had kept clear of most of the trouble that came his way. Not that he hadn't had his share, for times came when a man couldn't dodge fights. This could be that kind of time.

Dan Spencer was ramrodding the town. He was the big wheel. Milt had seen the big man's eyes trailing him down the dusty corner of road that did duty as Mesquite's main street. There were only four buildings on that street, and a dozen houses. Jennie lived in the house back under the cottonwoods with Joe and Mom Peters.

Spencer wasn't only big and rough. He was slick. He was slicker than blue mud on a side hill, only he didn't look it. Milt was a top hand at reading sign, and he could read the tracks years left across a man's face. He knew what manner of a man Dan Spencer was, and what to expect from the others, from Record and Martinez.

It was a mean little place, this valley. The scattering of ugly, unpainted frame buildings, the hillsides covered with scrub pine and juniper, the trail a dusty pathway through the pine and huge, flat-faced boulders. There was a waterhole, and it was that which had started the town. And somewhere back in the cliff and brush country there was a canyon where Spencer and his boys backed up their stolen cattle.

Thacker was right. He should throw a leg over his horse right now and light a shuck out of here. If he stayed, there would be trouble, and he was no gunfighter like Spencer or Record, nor a knife-in-the-belly killer like Martinez. He should light out of here right now, but there was Jennie Lewis.

Jennie was eighteen now, a slim, lovely girl

with soft gray eyes and ash-blond hair. She looked like the wind could blow her away but there was quick, bubbling laughter in her, and sometimes a look in her eyes that touched something away down inside of a man.

She was a casualty of the trail. Cholera had wiped out her family, and Joe Peters had found her, ten years old and frightened, and carried her home. Only now she was big enough and old enough for Spencer to see, and what Dan Spencer wanted, he took.

Nobody in town would stop Spencer. There were twenty-seven people in Mesquite, but those who weren't outlaws were shy, frightened people who made themselves obscure and came and went as silently as possible, fearful of speaking lest Dan Spencer lay eyes upon them.

———

That was how it had been until Milt Cogar rode into town with his catch of wild horses, sixteen head of them, and all fine stock, and most of them broke to ride. Milt was going on through, but he stopped by the waterhole with his horses, and while they drank he talked with Jennie.

"You've beautiful horses," she said wistfully. "I never saw anything so beautiful, not even the horses that Spencer has."

"They are nice." Cogar was a man unused to the sound of his voice, for he lived much alone. "That's one of the reasons why I catch them. I like working with horses."

She was standing near one of them, and the black put out a friendly nose, and she touched it. The horse did not shy.

"You would never guess they had ever been wild," she said wonderingly. "They are so gentle."

"Most horses are nice folks, ma'am," he said. "They like people. You teach one he doesn't have to be afraid, and right away he gets mighty curious and friendly. For the first few days you just keep them around, no sudden movements, no violence. Just keep a firm hand on them, and feed them well.

"Horses when frightened can't think, not even so much as people, but once they know a man, they'll trust him to take them anywhere at all."

She looked at him thoughtfully. "You must be a kind man," she said gently. "Most men around here break their horses rough."

He flushed and looked away, feeling the slow red on his face and neck and hating himself for being self-conscious. "I don't know about that, ma'am."

Hurriedly, he tried to change the subject. "Your folks live here?"

A shadow touched her face. "No, they are dead, long ago. I live with Joe Peters over on the sidehill. He and Mom took me in when I was a child." Her eyes went to his. "You aren't staying here?"

"I was figuring on drifting through," he said, "down toward the canyon country. I got me a little place down there, and I figured to rest up for a while."

"It must be nice to go wherever you want," she said slowly, shifting the heavy wooden bucket in her hands. "This is an awful place!"

The sudden feeling in her voice shocked him. "Why don't you leave?"

"I can't. Dan Spencer wouldn't let me, not even if I found a way to get out."

"Spencer? What's he to you?" Milt Cogar pushed his black hat back on his head and looked at her, seeing the softness in her eyes, and the worry, too. Yet it was more than worry: it was fear.

"He runs Mesquite and everybody in it. He . . . wants me."

"Do you want him? You aim to marry him?"

She flushed anew. "I've not much to say about it here. If he wants me, there's nobody to stop him. As for the rest of it, he hasn't said anything about marrying."

Milt Cogar felt chill anger rising within him.

"Who does this Spencer think he is?" he demanded. "Nobody can take a girl unless she wants to go! This country's free!"

"Not in Mesquite, it isn't! This is Dan Spencer's town, and nothing happens in it he don't like. You'd better keep him from seeing your horses, too. He'll want them."

"He'll trip himself up gettin' them!" Cogar said decisively. His eyes went to Jennie's face. "Ma'am, why don't you mount up and ride out of here? If you want to go, I'll see you get safe to the Ferry. Once across the river, you can head down toward Prescott or somewhere you'd be safe."

"Oh, if I only could—" Her voice died, and Milt looked up.

A burly, heavy-shouldered man with two guns was standing across the waterhole.

"If you could what?" the burly man asked. Then his eyes shifted to Milt, and from him to his horses, which he studied with a slow, appraising look, then back to Cogar. "Who are you?"

Milt looked at him with careful eyes. There was danger in this man, but he had faced danger before.

"I'm a man ridin' through," Milt said. "Who are you?"

Spencer stiffened. "Dan Spencer's the name, and I run this town."

Milt lifted his eyes insultingly toward the collection of miserable shacks. "Must keep you busy," he said.

"Not too busy but what I could teach you some manners!" Spencer's voice rang harshly. He walked around the waterhole, hands swinging at his sides. "Jennie, you go on home!"

Only an instant did the girl hesitate, apprehension for Cogar in her eyes. Then she began backing away.

Spencer stopped, a dozen feet from Milt, and dropped his hand to his gun butt—then the hand froze where it was, and Dan Spencer's eyes bulged. He was looking into the muzzle of a .44 Winchester carbine. "Unbuckle your belt, and be careful!" Milt warned.

Dan Spencer's face was gray. Very slowly he moved his fingers to the belt and unbuckled it, letting the Colts fall. "Now take a step toward me," Cogar commanded.

The big man complied. Color was coming back into his face and with it the realization that Milt Cogar had shown him up in front of the girl. Yet there was little he could do. His guns were on the ground behind him now.

"Now, let me tell you something, Spencer." Cogar spoke quietly, but coldly. "You let me alone. I'm passin' through Mesquite. I may decide to stay over a couple of days, but don't let that give you any ideas, because if you get tough with me, I'll kill you! Now pull your freight.''

When Spencer was gone, Milt stooped and shucked the shells from Spencer's guns, then from the belt, shoving the shells into his pocket—all but a few. He stood there by his horses and, taking out his knife, worked for a few minutes over those shells. Then he fed them back into the guns. When he was about to mount and ride on, he heard a low call from the brush. It was Jennie.

He mounted and rode over to where she waited, leaving his horses tied in groups of four.

''You'd better go quickly!'' she warned. ''He'll kill you! It isn't only him alone. He has other men. Two of them are John Record and Pablo Martinez. Both are killers and with him nearly all the time.''

Cogar looked down at the girl. He was a tall, spare man with a quiet, desert man's face.

''This is no place for a girl. You want to leave?'' he said.

Hope flashed into her eyes. ''Oh, I'd love to! But I've nowhere to go, and even if I wanted to, Spencer wouldn't allow it. Mom has wanted

Joe to smuggle me away, but he's afraid.''

"Well, you get back to your house and get together whatever you want to take along, but not much of it. You fix us a mite of grub, too. Then you slip out of the house, come daybreak, and meet me by that white boulder I can see just below town. I'll take you out of here, and see you get safe to help. You ain't afraid of me?''

Jennie looked at him quickly. "No, I guess not. You look like an honest man. Also I'm remembering you treat your horses kind. I trust you. Anyway,'' she added, "there's nobody else.''

He grinned. "That makes it simple. You be there, now. We may have to ride fast.''

When Milt Cogar had his horses bedded down on the edge of Mesquite, he studied the place warily. There was a saloon, a general store, a blacksmith shop, and an eating house. Leaving his carbine concealed near a clump of mesquite, he hitched his guns to an easier position and headed up the street. A heavy-bodied man with a stubble of beard showed on the saloon stoop. Milt avoided the place, rightly guessing it would be Spencer's hangout, and walked to the restaurant and went in.

A fat man with freckles and a fringe of sandy hair around a bald spot was cooking over an iron range. He glanced up.

"Fix me some grub," Milt suggested. "I'm sure hungry."

Red nodded briefly and, grabbing a big plate, ladled out a thick chunk of beef, a couple of scoops of beans, and some potatoes. Then he poured a cup of coffee from a battered coffee-pot and picked up some sourdough bread.

Cogar ate in silence for a while, then glanced up. "You one of Dan Spencer's outfit?"

Red stiffened. "I run my own shebang. If Spencer wants to eat, I feed him. That's all I have to do with him."

"I heard this was his town."

"It is. All but me." The door pushed open as he spoke, and Thacker came in. He sat down heavily on a chair across the table from Milt Cogar.

"Nice horses you got," he said tentatively.

Milt glanced up, taking in Thacker with a glance. "They'll do," he agreed.

"Don't need a hand, do you? Sixteen horses are a bunch for one man."

"My horses are gentle. I can handle them."

Thacker's face flushed a slow red, and he glanced toward the sandy-haired cook. He said softly:

"I could use a mite of work now. I'm sort of short."

Milt Cogar could sense the big man's embarrassment and it stirred his quick generosity. "Might lend you a bit," he suggested, keeping his own voice low. "Would ten dollars help?"

Thacker's face glowed red, but there was surprise and gratitude in his eyes. "I ain't no hand to borry," he said, "and you ridin' through like you are." He spoke hesitantly. "I reckon I hadn't better."

Cogar pushed a gold piece across the table. "Take it, man, and welcome. I've been staked a couple of times with no chance to pay back, so forget about paying me. When you have it, stake some other hombre."

When Thacker had gone, Red turned around. "Heard that," he said, then jerked his head toward the way Thacker had gone. "He ain't much good, either, but he's got him a boy he fair worships. He'll buy grub for that kid with the money, you can bank on it."

It was later, by the corral, that Thacker had come to Cogar with his warning. It was unnecessary, for Milt knew what he was facing. He also knew he was going to ride out of that town with Jennie Lewis or there would be blood on the streets. Yet he was no fighting man unless pushed. He wanted to get her away without trouble, yet when he faced the facts, he knew that Spencer grated on his nerves, that the thought

16

of the man ruling the helpless people of the town angered him.

Carefully, he looked over his horses, checking to see if any had injured feet, and stopping to talk and pet each one of them. They were fine stock, and would sell well, yet he never gentled a bunch like this without hating to part with them.

Up the street he could see lights going on in the saloon. He felt better with the meal under his belt, and he inspected his gun again. Spencer, Record, and Martinez, and half the town at least in cahoots with them. Nor could he expect any help. It was his game.

Milt backed up against a corral post and faced the town. He could watch from here. The horses liked to see him close. He dozed a little, knowing trouble would come later, if at all. For a while they would wait for him at the saloon, and that was a place he had no intention of going.

Darkness crawled over the hills and pushed patrols of shadow between the buildings and along the edge of the woods. More lights came on. Behind him a horse stamped and blew, and somewhere out on the desert, a blue quail called softly, inquiringly.

It was very quiet. A tin bucket rattled somewhere, and he could smell the oil on his guns.

17

Once he got up and walked among his horses, talking softly to them. His eyes shifted toward the light in the cabin where Jennie lived.

It seemed strange, having a woman to think about. He was a lonely man, and like so many lonely men he knew how to value love, attention, and the nearness of someone. He remembered the dusty spun gold of her hair, and the slim figure under the faded dress. There was something fine about her, something that spoke of another world than the world of Mesquite, Dan Spencer, and his followers.

He grinned ruefully. After all, she was not his to think about. He had only offered to help her, and once she was safely away—well, who was he to expect interest from such a girl as that?

A door opened and closed, and he glanced toward the saloon, making out a dark figure on the porch. The pale blotch above it was the man's face, looking toward him. Yet the watcher could not see Milt, for the blackness of his body would merge with the blackness of the corral corner.

They were beginning to wonder if he was coming, and when. He sat perfectly still, keeping his ears ready for the slightest sound. He did not look directly at the figure, but near it, and he did not allow his gaze to become fixed. He must be wary and ready always.

Had it not been for the weariness of his horses he might have started with Jennie at night, but the horses needed rest, and tomorrow would be a hard, long day. Doubly hard if Spencer elected to pursue.

The man on the porch returned inside, and Milt Cogar arose and moved around to get the stiffness from his muscles. Suddenly, an idea came to him, and he turned toward the corral, staring within. His own horses were outside, but inside were a half-dozen cow ponies used by Spencer and others. For an instant, Cogar considered, and then he got busy.

A sorrel with a white face had stayed close to the corral bars and several times he had patted it a little. Now he went inside and, catching the halter, led it out and tied it near his own horses. By soft talk and easy movements, he succeeded in getting two more outside where he tied them in plain view of the saloon. Then he took the first four of his own horses and, walking them carefully, led them away down the trail.

When he was out of sight of the town, he tied them and returned. In four trips he had led all of his own horses to the same place. Then he untied the first four, knowing they would stay together. After that he walked back and saddled his gray gelding. The paint he had caught earlier was already saddled and waiting. He had bought the extra saddle from a busted cowhand down Las Vegas way, but now it was to come in handy.

He retrieved his rifle and slid it into the scabbard. Then he sat down and lit a cigarette. Twice in the next hour or so a man came to the saloon door and looked out. Each time he let the cigarette glow brightly.

From where he sat he could see the corner of the water trough in the corral, and a glow caught his eye. For a few minutes he studied it curiously, and then recognized it. The glow was that greenish, phosphorescent light from damp, rotten wood, such as he had often seen in swampy country, or after a period of heavy rains. Many times he had seen branches like that, greenish, ghostly fingers reaching into the darkness.

It gave him another idea and he got to his feet again and walked off a short distance. It was still visible. This would be just the added touch he would need to make his escape effective. He broke off a small bit of the wood and fastened it into the corral post where he had been sitting, and then moved out into the street. The glow was still visible, not so bright as a cigarette, but enough to fool anyone taking a casual glance toward the corral. They were, he was sure, waiting for him to fall asleep.

Once the phosphorescent wood was in place, he moved swiftly. Getting into the saddle, he led the gray horse behind him and moved across the valley toward the Peters cabin, where Jennie Lewis lived. Dismounting then, he concealed his horses in the timber, and moved up to the house. A quick glance through the windows, and he saw no one but Jennie, carrying dishes away from the table, and the two older people.

Stepping up to the back door, he tapped gently. There was a moment of silence within, then a question. "Who is it?" At his reply, the door opened and he stepped inside.

"We've got to go now," he said quickly. "My horses aren't ready for it, but Spencer's bunch are watching me, and we've got a chance to get away that may give us an hour or so of start."

Joe Peters was staring at him, his face pale. "Hope you make it!" he said. "I hate to think what Spencer will do when we don't tell him you're gone! He's apt to kill us both, or whup us!"

"We'll fix that," Cogar replied. "We'll tie you both. You can say I threw a gun on you."

"Sure!" Peters said. "Sure thing!" He turned to his wife, "Mom, you let me tie you, and then this hombre can tie me."

21

Jennie had not hesitated. When he spoke she had turned and gone into her room, and now she came out. Startled, he saw she had a pistol belt around her hips.

"Pa's gun," she said, at his question. "It might come in handy!"

They rode swiftly until they reached the edge of the settlement, and then swung around toward where Milt Cogar had left his horses. As they drew alongside, Milt got down to unfasten the ropes that tied them in groups of four. They might have to run, and he wanted nothing to tangle them up.

Suddenly, a dark figure moved from the shadow of the mesquite, and a low voice spoke softly. "I've got you covered. If you move I'll shoot!"

It was not Dan Spencer. But Record, perhaps?

"Who's moving?" he said calmly. "You're doin' a fool thing, buttin' in on this deal."

"Am I?" The man stepped out from the darkness of the mesquite, and Cogar could see his face. The man was slim, wiry, and hard-jawed. The gun he held brooked no argument. "Anyway, I'm in. Dan Spencer will be pleased to find I've stopped you from gettin' away with his girl."

Milt Cogar held himself very still. There was only one way he could come out of this alive, and it required a gamble with his life at stake. The moment would come. In the meanwhile, he tried the other way, for which he had no hope.

"Folks won't let you steal this girl," he said. "They'll stand for everything but that."

"They'll stand for that, too," the man said. "Now turn around!"

"Stay where you are!" Jennie's voice was low, penetrating. "Johnny Record, I've got you covered. Drop that gun or I'll kill you!"

Record stiffened, but before he could realize that as long as Cogar was covered there was a stalemate, the girl's voice snapped again.

"You drop that gun before I count three or I'll shoot! One! Two! Thr—"

Her count ended as Record let go of his gun. Milt stepped up and retrieved it. Swiftly then, he spun Record around and tied him tightly, hand and foot.

In the saddle and moving away, he glanced through the darkness toward Jennie. "I reckon as a hero I don't count for much, you gettin' us out of that fix!"

"What else could I do? Anyway, I'd never have had the courage unless you were taking me away like this. With a man to help, I'm brave enough, I guess."

———

They rode on, holding a steady if not fast pace. There was small chance of them losing any pursuit. That would have to be met when it came. He couldn't leave his horses behind, for they were all he had. He might need the money from their sale to help Jennie. She would be friendless and alone.

The desert was wide and white in the moonlight, with only the dark, beckoning fingers of the giant cactuses or the darker blotches of the mesquite or distant mountains. He turned off the trail he had been following, heading into the canyon country. This would be rough going, but there were places ahead where one might stand off an army.

Foothills crept out into the desert toward them, and they started the horses into a deep draw between two parted arms of hills. The rock walls grew higher and higher, and they lost the light, having only a small rectangle of starlit sky overhead. Milt took no time to rest, but pushed the horses relentlessly, taking no time for anything but getting on.

He knew where he was going, and he knew he must make it by daylight. Jennie said nothing, but he could sense her weariness, judging it to an extent by his own, for her strength would not be equal to his.

Finally, the canyon opened out into a wide

flat valley in the mountains, and he moved the horses into the tall grass, giving them no rest, but pushing them diagonally across it. They were mounting toward the far wall of the valley before he drew up.

"We'll stop here, Jennie," he said, "but we daren't have a fire."

He divided the blankets and rolled up in his. In a moment, he was sound asleep. He was unworried about the horses, for they would be too tired to go far.

The sun on his face awakened him, and he came to a sitting position with a start. Jennie was sitting about a dozen feet away with his rifle across her knees.

Milt stared at her, red-faced. "I slept like a tenderfoot!" he said, abashed.

"I'm not used to sleeping out, so I awakened early, that's all. There was no need you being awake. Anyway, they just came into the valley."

"Spencer?"

"Three of them. They came out of the ravine over there and are scouting for our trail. They haven't found it yet."

"Probably not. There's wild horses in this valley and their herd tracks are everywhere." Jennie looked tired but her eyes were bright. "We'll saddle up and get going."

When they were moving again, he hugged the wall of the canyon, knowing they would scarcely be visible against its darkness. They pushed on steadily, and from time to time his eyes strayed to the girl. She rode easily in the saddle, her willowy body yielding to every movement of the horse.

He found he liked having her there. He had never realized how nice it was to know there was someone beside you, someone who mattered. That was the trouble. It was going to be lonesome when she was gone. To avoid that thought, he turned in his saddle and glanced back. They were coming, all three of them, and he had no more than a mile or two of leeway before they would catch up.

Milt's mind was quick, and he knew this valley. The hollow up ahead was the only possible chance. He rode up and turned the horses into it, backing them into the trees along the hillside out of range. Jennie had followed his glance when he looked back, and her face was pale.

When the horses were safely under the trees, he walked back to the crest of the rise. It was a poor place for defense, yet nothing else offered. In the bottom of the hollow one was safely out of range unless they circled around and got on the mountain behind it. If that happened, there

26

would be small chance for either of them. Still, Milt thought as he nestled down into the grass, there were only three outlaws.

They came on, riding swiftly, and he knew they had seen the two of them ride into the hollow. Jennie moved up beside him.

"I can load your rifle," she whispered, "while you stand them off with the six-guns."

He nodded to indicate he understood, and lifted the .44 Winchester. When they were within rifle range, he sighted at them, then took the gun from his shoulder and let them come closer. At last he lifted the rifle again and put a shot into the ground ahead of them. They drew up.

"That won't get you no place!" Spencer roared. "You turn that girl loose and we'll let you go!"

Cogar made no reply, merely waiting. There was some talk down below, and then he called out. "You've come far enough. Don't advance any further!"

One of them, probably Martinez, although Milt could not be sure, wheeled his horse and started for the hollow at a dead run. Milt lifted the rifle and fired.

The rifle leaped in his hand, and Martinez yelled and threw up his hands. He went off the horse as it veered sharply and cut away across the grass. Martinez staggered to his feet and, one arm hanging limp, started back toward the other two outlaws.

Cogar let him go. He was not a killer, and wanted only to be let alone.

Four more horsemen were coming up, and were scarcely more than a half mile away. They came on, and drew up with Spencer, where they began to talk.

"That makes six of them out there, not counting Martinez," Cogar said. "Looks like we're in for it."

"You could let them have me," Jennie suggested. Her cheek was pillowed on her forearm, and her wide eyes on his face.

He did not take his eyes from them. "Don't talk foolishness! I said I'd take you away, and I will. My promises are good."

"Is your promise the only reason?"

"Maybe it is and maybe it ain't. Womenfolks always have to see things personal-like. If you can be got out of this alive, I'll get you out."

"You know, you're really quite good-looking."

"Huh?" He looked around, startled at the incongruous remark. Then as it hit him, he flushed.

"Oh, forget it! Looks ain't gettin' us out of this hole! What I'm afraid of is they'll get somebody on the mountain behind us, or else they'll fire the grass.''

''Fire the grass?'' Her head jerked up and her face went white. ''Oh, no! They wouldn't burn us!''

''That outfit? They'd do anything if they got good and riled.''

Some sort of a plan seemed to have been arrived at. Dan Spencer shouted again:

''One more chance! Come out with your hands up and we'll turn you loose! Otherwise we're comin' after you!''

They were barely within rifle range, and Milt Cogar knew the chips were down. His reply was a rifle shot that clipped a white hat from the head of a newcomer. They all hit dirt then.

''I wanted to get him then,'' Milt muttered. ''That wasn't to scare him.''

Milt was scared, he admitted to himself. He was as scared as he'd ever been, yet in another way, he wasn't. There was no way out that he could see, and if they fired the grass the only chance was a run for the horses and a wild break in an attempt to outrun the attackers. But there was small chance of that working, for there were too many of them. An idea came suddenly.

''You slip back there,'' he said. ''Get the

horses down into the hollow. We may have to make a break for it.''

She glanced at him quickly, and then without a word, slid back down the slope and got to her feet. He heard a rifle spang, but what happened to the bullet, he didn't know, and then there was a volley and he knew what happened to all the rest. Two whipped by right over his head, and one of them burned him across the shoulders. He rolled over and crept to another position. He could see nothing to shoot at, yet a moment later there was a movement down below, and he fired twice, fast as he could lever the rifle.

The movement stopped, and he rolled over again, getting himself to a new position. If they got to the edge of the hollow, he was done for, but he couldn't watch all the terrain. A bullet nipped the grass over his head and he fired at the sound.

Stealing a quick glance backward, he saw Jennie coming out of the trees into the hollow with the horses. They seemed disturbed by the firing, and halted not far away.

Spencer yelled then, and instantly, without replying, Milt snapped a shot at the spot, then one left and one right of it. He heard a startled yelp, but doubted from the sound that his shot had more than burned the renegade.

"Get to your horse but keep your head down!" he warned Jennie. "Now listen: we're going out of here, you and I, and fast when we go. We're going to start our horses right down there into the middle of them, and try to crash through. It's a wild chance, but from the way they act, they are scattering out to get all around us. If they do, we won't have much chance. If we run for it now, right at them, they may get us, but we'll have a chance of stampeding their horses."

He swung into the saddle and they turned the herd of fifteen horses toward the enemy, then with whoops and yells, started them on a dead run for Spencer. The rim of the hollow and the tall grass gave them a few precious moments of invisibility, so when the horses went over the rise they were at a dead run.

Milt Cogar, a six-gun in each hand, blazed away over the heads of the horses at the positions of the attackers. He saw instantly that he had been right, for men were already moving on foot off to left and right to surround the hollow.

With a thunder of racing hoofs, the horses charged down on Spencer's position, nostrils flaring, manes flowing in the wind of their furious charge.

Milt saw Dan Spencer leap to his feet and

throw up a gun, but his shot went wild, and the next instant he turned and fled. Johnny Record had started to move off to the right, but he turned when he saw the charging horses, and threw his rifle to his shoulder. Cogar snapped a shot at him, and the yells of the men ahead swerved the horses.

There was a moment of startled horror as Record saw death charging upon him, and then he dropped his rifle and started to run. He never made it, and Milt heard his death scream as he went down under the lashing hoofs. And then the herd was racing away down the valley.

"Milt!" Jennie's cry was agonized.

He swung his horse and looked back. The gray had fallen with her, spilling her over on the ground even as she screamed. And running toward her was Dan Spencer.

Milt Cogar's horse was beside her in three bounds and he dropped from the saddle, drawing as he hit ground. His first shot was too quick, and he missed. Spencer skidded to a halt, his face triumphant.

"Now we'll see!" he shouted.

The veins swelled in his forehead, and his eyes were pinpoints of steel. His gun bucked in his hand, and Milt's leg went out from under him, but even as his knee hit ground, he fired. His bullet caught Spencer in the diaphragm, and knocked him back on his heels. Both men fired again, but Dan Spencer's shot bit into the earth just in front of Cogar, and he thumbed his gun, aiming low down at the outlaw's body. Spencer backed up, his jaw working, his eyes fiercely alive. Then a bloody froth came to his lips, and Milt, cold and still inside, fired once more. The outlaw's knees gave way and he pitched over on his face.

Milt stared at the fallen man, fumbling at his belt for more cartridges. His fingers seemed very clumsy, but he finally filled the empty chambers. Jennie was hobbling toward him.

"I've sprained my ankle," she said, "but it's nothing!"

She dropped beside him, and gasped when she saw the blood on his trouser leg. "You're hurt!" she exclaimed.

"Not much," he told her. "Who's that coming?"

Her head came up sharply. Then her face whitened with relief. "It's Joe Peters! And Thacker!"

The two men walked up, the slender Peters looking even smaller beside the rope-girthed bulk of Thacker. Both men had rifles.

"You two all right?" Thacker demanded. The hesitation and fear seemed to have left him. "We hurried after you to help, but we got here late."

"What happened to the other men with Spencer?" Cogar asked.

"The horses got both Martinez and Record. We found one other man dead, one wounded. We kilt one our ownselves, and caught up the rest."

Red came up. "Reckon you started somethin', mister," he said to Milt. "When you took Jennie away so's Spencer couldn't have her, we decided it was right mean of us to let a stranger protect our women. So Thacker here, he seen Joe Peters, and a few others. Then we got together at my eatin' place and started cleanin' the town. We done a good job!"

Thacker grinned, well pleased with himself. "You two can come back if you want," he suggested. "This here deserves a celebration."

"Why, I'd like to come back, sometime," Milt said, "but right now I've got to get my horses down to my own ranch and into the pasture there. I'd take Jennie to see the place, if she'll go."

"A ranch might be nice," Jennie said. Her eyes smiled at him, but there was something grave and serious in their depths. "I might like it."

"Only if you come, I might want to keep

you,'' Milt said. ''It isn't going to be the same after this.''

''Why should it?'' Jennie said.

The gray had gotten to his feet and was shaking himself. Milt walked over to him, and his hand trembled as he examined the gelding's legs. When he straightened up, Jennie was facing him, and her lips looked soft and inviting.

''I reckon,'' Thacker said, pleased, ''that we'll have to celebrate without them!''

Love and
the Cactus Kid

Author's Note

Nowadays when we see women riding in the West they're usually wearing blue jeans, but this was not the case during the time these stories take place. Up until World War I, or shortly thereafter, a woman wouldn't have been caught dead wearing pants anywhere. She wore a dress wherever she went.

Women never rode a horse astride unless they were miles from where anybody was likely to see them. Then they might. They rode sidesaddle, and sidesaddle only, with the dress very carefully draped over the side of the horse. I had an aunt, a very beautiful young woman, who rode that way, and she was something to watch.

In public a woman was very careful not to show any more than her ankles. And about the only time you got to see them was when she was getting out of a stage or down off a railroad train.

Chapter I
Flowers for Jenny

Jenny Simms, who was pocket-sized and lovely, lifted her determined chin. "If you loved me, you would! You know you would! It's just that you don't love me enough! Why, just look at what the knights used to do for their ladies! And you won't even get me some flowers!"

"Flowers?" The Cactus Kid stared at her gloomily. "Now it's flowers! Girls sure do beat me! Where in this country would a man find flowers?"

His wave at the surrounding country where their picnic lunch was spread was expressive and definite. "Look at it! Ain't been a drop of rainfall in four months, and you know it! Scarcely a blade of grass that's even part green! Worst drought in years, and you want flowers!"

"If you loved me you'd get them!" Her voice was positive and brooked no argument. "If a man really loves a girl he can do anything!"

Her blue eyes flashed at him, and their beauty shook him anew. "Nesselrode, if you love me . . . !"

"Sssh!" he pleaded, glancing panic-stricken around. "If anybody heard that name they'd hooraw me out of the country. Call me Clay, or Kid, or anything but Nesselrode!"

"It's your name, isn't it? Nesselrode Clay. I see nothing wrong with it, nothing at all! Furthermore"—she was not to be diverted—"if you love me you'll get me some flowers! I told the girls you were giving me flowers and they laughed at me! They did. They said there were no flowers closer than California, this time of year."

The Cactus Kid rolled a smoke and stared at it with dark disgust. Women! He snorted. What they could think of! Jenny could think of things nobody else would dream of. That came of reading so many books, all romances and the like. Made her look for a man on a white charger who would do great feats to win her love.

Not that he wouldn't. Why right now, instead of being on a picnic with Jenny, he ought to be out with the posse chasing the Herring boys. There were three of them, and all were gun-slick and tough. They had stopped the U.P. train on a grade about fifteen miles from here, killed the express messenger and the fireman. They had looted the safe of forty thousand dollars in gold and bills. There was a reward on them, a thousand apiece for Benny and Joe, and four thousand for Red.

With the money he could buy some cows and stock that little ranch he was planning on. He could set up a home for a girl like Jenny to be proud of, and with his know-how about cows they could soon be well off. But no, instead of hunting for the Herrings, she wanted him to go hunt flowers!

"It's little enough to do for me," she persisted. "All you think of is running around shooting people in the stomach! You ought to be ashamed, Nesselrode!"

He winced and started to speak, but his voice was lost in the storm of words.

"If you don't bring me some flowers for my birthday, Nesselrode, I'll never speak to you again! Never!"

"Aw, honey!" he protested. "Don't be like that! The sheriff asked me particular to go along and hunt for the Herrings. The boys'll think I'm scared!"

"Nesselrode Clay! You listen to me! If you don't get me those flowers, I never want to see you again! And don't you be shooting anybody, either! Every time you go to do something for me you get into trouble, shooting somebody in the stomach!''

Jenny Simms was five feet one inch of dark-haired loveliness and fire. Almost, sometimes, the Cactus Kid wished there were less of the fire. At other times, he welcomed it.

The fact that she was the prettiest girl in four counties, that her five feet one inch was firm, shapely, and trim as a two-year-old filly, all conspired to make the Kid cringe at the thought of losing her. He was, unfortunately, in love, and the male animal in love is an abject creature when faced by the tyranny of his beloved. At the time he should be firm, he is weak. At the time he should have been getting her accustomed to driving in harness he was so much in love that he was letting her get the bit in her teeth.

The Cactus Kid, five feet seven inches of solid muscle and bone, curly-haired and given to smiling with a charm all his own, was the most sought-after young man around. At the moment, nobody would have guessed. Nor would they have guessed that the black-holstered, walnut-stocked .44's hanging just now on his saddle were considered by some to be the fastest and deadliest guns in the Rocky Mountain country.

''All right,'' he said weakly, ''I'll get your

flowers. Come hell or high water, I'll get 'em!'' He gave her his hands and helped her up from the flat rock where she was sitting.

———

Away from the flashing beauty of Jenny's eyes, he was no longer so confident. Flowers! There wasn't a water hole in fifteen miles that wasn't merely cracked earth and gray mud. The streams had stopped running two months ago. Cattle were dying, all that hadn't been hurriedly sold off, and the leaves on the trees had turned crisp and brown around the edges.

Flowers! He scowled thoughtfully. The Widow Finnegan had a garden, and usually there were flowers in bloom. Now maybe . . .

The piebald gelding with the pink nose and pink-rimmed eyes was a fast horse on the road, and it moved fast now, going through the hills toward the Slash Five and the Widow Finnegan's elm-shaded yard. Yet long before he reached it he could see that even the elms looked parched and bare.

The Widow Finnegan was five feet ten and one hundred and eighty pounds of Irishwoman and she met him at the gate.

"Not here!" She looked about as approachable as a bulldog with a fresh bone. "Not here you don't be gettin' no flowers, Kid!"

"Why, I . . . ." His voice trailed away under the pale blue of her glaring eyes.

"There'll be no soft-soapin' me, nayther!" the Widow Finnegan said sharply. "I know the likes of you, Cactus Kid! Full of blarney an' honey-tongued as a thrush! But I know all about the flowers ye'll be wantin', an' there's few enough left, an' them withered!"

"You . . . heard of it?" he asked.

"Heard of it? An' hasn't that colleen o' yours been sayin' all aboot that ye were bringin' her flowers for her birthday! Flowers enough to decorate the rooms with? Flowers in this country where a body is that lucky to find a green blade of grass?"

He glanced thoughtfully at the fence around the small patch of flowers, most of them looking very sick from the hot winds and no rain. She caught his look, and flared.

"No, ye don't! I'm not to be fooled by the likes of ye, Cactus Kid! Ye come back here at night an' every hand on the Slash Five will be digging rock salt out of your southern exposure! An' it's not just talkin' I am!"

———

A half-dozen men loafed in the High Card Saloon and they all looked up when he shouldered through the door.

"Rye!" he said.

"What's the matter?" Old Man Hawkins leered at him. "Ain't you after the Herrings? Or have they got you buffaloed too?"

The Cactus Kid looked at him with an unfriendly eye. "Got to get some flowers for Jenny," he said lamely, "and she's fussing about me getting into shooting scrapes."

" 'S the way with women," the barkeep said philosophically. "Fall for a man, then set out to change him. Soon's they got him changed they don't like him no more. Never seen it to fail, Kid."

"Speakin' of flowers," Sumner suggested, "I hear tell there's a gent over to Escalante that orders 'em shipped in."

"Be all dried up," the barkeep objected. "Jenny'll want fresh flowers."

"Ain't goin' to find none!" Old Man Hawkins said cheerfully. "Might's well give up, Kid, an' hightail it after the Herrings. You would at least git some money if you got them . . . *if* you got 'em."

The Cactus Kid stared malevolently at his unoffending drink. Meanwhile he tried to arrange his thoughts into some sort of order. Now, flowers. Where would a man be apt to find flowers? Nowhere on the flatland, that was

47

sure. The grass was dried up or the season wrong for any kind he knew of.

A man got up and walked to the bar and stopped beside the Kid. He was a big old man wearing a greasy buckskin shirt.

"I'm Ned Hayes," he said, "prospector. Heard you talkin' about flowers. You'll find plenty in the Blue Mountains. Ain't no drought up thataway. Country shore is green an' purty."

"Thanks." The Kid straightened up, suddenly filled with hope. Then he hesitated, remembering Jenny's admonition about fighting. "Ain't any trouble down thataway, is there? I sure aim to keep out of it this trip."

Hayes chuckled. "Why, man, you won't see a living soul! Nobody ever goes down there 'cept maybe a drifting Injun. Robbers' Roost is some north, but they never git down so far. No, you won't see a soul, but you better pack extra grub. There's game, but you won't find no cattleman an' nary a sheep camp. I never seen nobody."

———

The eight peaks of the mountain group were black against the sky when the Cactus Kid's first day on the trail was ending. This was rough, wild, wind-worried and sun-scorched country, all new to him. Its wild and majestic beauty was lonely as a plateau on the moon, and water was scarce. He pushed on, remembering that Ned Hayes had said there was no drought in the Blues and not wanting to pitch dry camp out on the escarpment.

"Grassy on the east slopes, Kid," Hayes had added. "What yuh'll want to do is to cross the Divide. That is, go over the ridge to the west slope, and there you'll find the greenest forest you ever saw, rushing mountain streams, an' a passel of wild flowers of all kinds and shapes."

All day he had seen no track of horse or man, not even the unshod track of an Indian pony. It was eerie, lonely country and the Kid found himself glancing uneasily over his shoulder and staring in awed wonder at the eight peaks. The mountains were new to him, and they comprised a large section of country, all of sixteen miles long and about ten across.

The piebald was climbing now, and he bent to it with a will. The Kid had stumbled upon the semblance of a trail, an ancient Indian route, probably not used in centuries. It was marked at intervals by small piles of stones such as used to mark their trails in the deserts farther west.

The horse liked it. He could smell the rich, nutritious grass, and was ducking his head for an occasional mouthful. He had no idea where this strange master of his was taking him, but it looked like horse country. Grouse flew up from under his feet, and once a couple of black-tailed deer darted away from his movement, then stopped not a dozen yards away to study him.

Before him the hills showed a notch that seemed to offer a pass to the farther side, and the Cactus Kid swung his horse that way. Then he reined in sharply and stared at the ground.

Three hard-ridden horses had cut in sharply from the north, then swung toward the same cut in the hills that he was heading for. And the trail was fresh!

"What d' you know?" the Cactus Kid muttered. "Riders in this country! Well, nothing like company!"

Yet he rode more warily, for well he knew that riders in such an area might be on the dodge. North and west of here was a district in the canyons already becoming famous as Robbers' Roost, and strange bands of horses or cattle occasionally drifted through the country, herded by hard-eyed riders who kept their own counsel and avoided trails.

Chapter II
A Red Herring

Shadows were gathering into black pools in the canyons when he finally saw the notch in the hills deepen into a real opening. The piebald, weary as he was, walked now with his ears cocked forward, and once the Cactus Kid was quite sure he smelled dust in the air.

Despite the heat of the day, the evening grew chill and the night would be cold. The atmosphere was thin here, and the altitude high, yet he wanted to go over the pass before he bedded down. His eyes and ears were alert for sight or sound of the riders who preceded him, but he heard nothing, saw nothing.

At last he rode into the deep shadows of an aspen grove and, hearing water, pushed toward it. Here, on the banks of a small stream, he found a hollow. He built a fire, carefully shielded, and picketed his horse. After a brief supper and coffee, he rolled in his blanket and poncho and slept the night through.

He awoke to find his fire only the soft gray of wood ashes, the sky of the same shade and texture. Chilled, he threw off his blankets and built a fire of mountain mahogany, young pine, and branches broken from the dead lower limbs

51

of the aspen. Soon the fire was crackling and he had water on.

The morning was still and cold. Below him the tops of trees were like islands in the mist rising from the forest, a thick fog like the smoke of leaf fires. The air was damp and the smoke held low, but the hungry tongues of the fire ate rapidly at the dry branches. In a matter of minutes there was the smell of coffee and of beef frying.

Several times he walked away from the task of preparing breakfast to look out through the woods beyond the hollow in which he was camped. Without any reason, he felt uneasy and his mind kept returning to the three riders. No honest men would be in this country unless they were passing through, and there were easier routes to the east and north. He thought of the Herrings but dismissed it at once. They were east of here and by now the posse probably had them.

His breakfast over, he led the piebald to water, but the horse refused to drink from the cold stream. Quickly he saddled up, then mounted. The black-and-white horse pitched a few times in a casual, disinterested way, more as a matter of form than of conviction. The Kid moved out.

Almost at once he saw the flowers. Many of

them were sego lilies, faintly orchid in these mountains rather than pure white. There were other flowers, mostly of purple or violet colors, shading to white and some to blue. Lilac sunbonnet, forget-me-not, chia, and many other flowers seemed to be blooming here, most of which he knew but slightly or from the Indian use of some of them as remedies or food.

Sighting a particularly thick field of flowers, the Cactus Kid swung from his saddle and started into the field. He had stooped to pick flowers when a hard voice spoke behind him.

"Hold it right there, sprout," the voice said unpleasantly, "or you get a Winchester slug in your spine."

The Kid froze, startled but puzzled. "What's the matter?" he asked mildly. "I ain't troubling nobody."

"You ain't goin' to, neither." This was another voice. "What you doin' here?"

"Came after some flowers for my girl," the Kid said, realizing as he spoke that it sounded ridiculous.

A big man lumbered around in front of him, glancing at his face. "Yeah, you're right, Red. It's him. It's the Cactus Kid, all right. Shucks, I figured him quite a man from all I heard! This one's only a sprout."

"I don't like that word," the Kid said coldly.

"Who are you, and what do you want with me?"

The big man chuckled. "Hear that, Red? He don't like being called sprout, an' he's only up here pickin' flowers! Now, ain't that sweet?"

The man guffawed, then sobered suddenly and struck the Kid a wicked, backhand blow that knocked him to the ground. The Kid, fury rising in him and throttling his good sense, grabbed for his guns. Instantly, a hawk-faced red-haired man confronted him and there was no arguing with the rifle in his hands.

"Drop it, Kid! We hear you're mighty fast on the draw, but you ain't that fast!"

Reluctantly, the Cactus Kid lifted his hands away from the guns and raised them shoulder high.

"Keep that big lug off me, then," he protested, "or else take my guns and turn me loose! I'll tear down his meat house!"

"Why, you dumb sprout!" The big man started forward. "I got a notion to . . . . !"

"Cut it out!" Red said angrily. "What's the matter, Joe? You lettin' him get your goat? Forget it." The red-haired man turned his cold gray eyes on the Kid. "Who's with you?"

"Nobody! I come up here alone, and like I said, I'm after *flowers*."

"Flowers!" Joe sneered. "He's after flowers! Now, wouldn't that kill you? The Cactus Kid, gunfighter and manhunter, after *flowers!*"

The Kid glared. "I'll peel your hide for this, you buttonheaded maverick!"

"Shut up!" Red spoke harshly. "Get along toward that dead fir. Right over there! Joe"— Red's voice was sharp—"bring that piebald. We can use a good horse."

"You aiming to set me afoot?" The Kid spoke more quietly. "Look, Red Whatever-your-name-is, I'm on the level about this flower business. My gal down to Helper, she's giving a party. You know how women are."

"How are they?" Red questioned. "I ain't talked to a woman in three months. You keep movin', an' watch your talk to Joe an' Benny. They get mighty touchy."

Joe and Benny . . . and Red.

The Herring brothers!

———

He was so startled he almost missed his footing and fell, but caught himself in time. Of course! What had he been thinking of not to guess at once who they were? Joe and Benny Herring, killers both of them, wanted for bank and train holdups, but nothing at all to the deadly Red Herring, the gunman from the Gila. A cold-blooded and vicious killer with a flashing speed that had sent more than one marshal and sheriff to boot hill.

The Herrings . . . and they had him cold turkey. The boys who had forced a banker to open the bank safe, then escort them from town, and on the outskirts had coolly shot him dead.

And Jenny had warned him against getting into a fight. He groaned, and Red Herring prodded him with a rifle barrel.

"What's that for?" he demanded.

"Aw, Jenny . . . she's my girl. She warned me not to get in any fights."

Red chuckled without humor. "Don't worry, cowhand, you ain't in no fight, nor liable to be. You lost this one afore it started. Frankly, we'd as soon hang your hide on the cabin wall as rob a bank. We heard of you."

The Kid decided nothing was to be gained by conversation. He had no doubt Red meant just what he said. They might have had friends, if such men ever had friends, whom he had gunned down or helped send over the road to the pen. Anyway, in outlaw hangouts the killing of the Cactus Kid would be something to boast about.

Suddenly the earth broke sharply off in a thick grove of aspen where a steep, rocky trail wound downward through the trees. It was a one-man-at-a-time trail, and when they reached the bottom they were in a nest of boulders mingled with ancient trees, huge white-limbed deadfalls, and the sound of running water.

Benny Herring was a thin, saturnine man with a scar on his chin. He looked up at them, staring at the Kid.

"He the one followed us?" He stared evilly at the Kid. "How'd you spot our trail? Who else knows about it?"

"He says he come up here huntin' flowers!" Joe sneered.

Benny eyed him without humor or interest. "What did you bring him back for? Why didn't you shoot him an' leave him lay?"

"Buzzards." Red's voice was casual. "Tie him up, Joe."

"Sure." Joe shambled up to him, grinning out of his narrow eyes. Then he smashed the Kid across the face, over and back, caught him before he fell, and shoved him against a stunted tree scarcely taller than the Kid himself.

The Cactus Kid felt blood trickling down his chin, and he glared at Joe, taking a deep breath. Joe tied him tightly and thoroughly. Then he stared at the Kid, who stared back at him. Setting himself, Joe hooked a right to his wind and the Kid felt his breath leave him with a gasp.

Without a backward glance, Joe Herring

slouched to the fire and the three began eating, talking in a low-voiced, desultory fashion. Despite their questions about who else knew of their trail, they seemed unworried, so the Kid deduced they had actually seen him behind them on the previous day, and knew he was alone.

He was no fool. His situation was desperate. That they would not hesitate to leave him dead, he knew. All three of these men would hang if caught alive and they had proved too many times in the past that they had no hesitation about killing a helpless man. None of them was the sort to be troubled by qualms or conscience.

Red was obviously the leader, yet from his looks Benny was no fool. Joe was a hulking brute, physically powerful, but mentally his range was bare.

The Kid's chances looked nil, and they might kill him at any time. However, if they would leave him alone for a while . . . He had his own ideas about that, and his first ruse had worked.

Red had said they did not kill him because of buzzards. They were afraid attention might be drawn to the area by some chance rider seeing circling buzzards. That implied they were not ready to leave. For all he knew, this area might be a permanent hideout for them, and might explain why they had so often dropped from sight on previous occasions.

Tentatively, he tried his bonds. Having taken a deep breath and swelled his muscles before being tied, he now had a little slack. It was little enough, but he was thankful that he had not been hit in the wind before being tied, as that little slack might make all the difference in the world. His four inches of chest expansion had been a help before this, but never had he needed it so much.

His wrists, however, were tightly bound, although he knew he could move around the tree with some ease if left alone.

When they finished eating, Benny mounted a horse and drifted out of the hollow—to act as a lookout, the Kid guessed. Red smoked a cigarette and eyed the Kid irritably. Obviously, he was in the way, and wouldn't be kept around for long.

Red Herring was wise in not attracting attention to their hideout, for the Cactus Kid knew that searchers were not even coming this way, and as this country was seldom traveled, it was perfection itself for their purposes. There was small chance that anyone might see the circling buzzards, but at this time caution was the smart thing and Red Herring had the cunning of a wolf. At the same time, the Kid knew that it would serve no purpose to keep him alive. He was only an encumbrance, and the sooner they rid themselves of him the better off they were.

An idea came to the Kid suddenly, an idea that might keep him alive a little longer, and he desperately wanted to live.

"You got it mighty good here," he said. "Only that money won't do you much good in this hole."

"We don't aim to stay." Red threw a couple of dry sticks on the fire. "Just to let things quiet down."

"They'll be watching for you at Hanksville, Greenriver, and Dandy Crossing. At Helper and Henrieville, too."

Herring looked up, studying the Kid. "How'd you know that?"

"They wanted me in the posse. I wouldn't go because my girl wanted the flowers."

Red grunted. "You stickin' to that story? Why come way down here?"

"Figure it out for yourself. With this drought there ain't none anywhere around. Prospector told me about these flowers. Hombre name of Hayes."

Red nodded. "Know about him. So they got us bottled up, have they? Why tell us? Why not let us ride into a trap?"

The Kid grinned wryly. "Because I want to live. To get you killed after I'm dead doesn't help me, and the way I figure it, you don't aim to let me live that long."

"That's right. We'll kill you before the day's out. Drop you in a hole over west of here. Still, I don't see why you tell me."

"I said, because I want to live . . . and there's a way out of this country."

"Out of here? How?" The Kid was aware of Red's awakened interest. If he could keep him hooked . . .

"South of here, if you know the water holes. Otherwise, you can die out there."

"South?" Red studied the situation. "That's a mighty long ride. I heard a man couldn't make it through. You know the water holes?"

"Sure, I know 'em. And I know the trails like an Injun. You boys aren't known down thataway, either, are you?"

Red got to his feet and walked over, rolling a smoke. He stuck the cigarette in the Kid's lips and lit it.

"No, we ain't." He studied the Kid carefully. "You figure we'll let you go if you take us through?"

The Kid grinned. "No. I never heard of you doing anybody any favors, Red. But the longer I stay alive the better my chances are. You might decide to lay off, or I might get a chance to light a shuck.''

Red chuckled but without humor. ''Yeah, that's reasonable enough. You're buying time.''

Chapter III
Desperate Chance

Nothing more was said and they waited the hours out. The men changed jobs from time to time, and there was much low-voiced discussion among them. As the night drew on, it became rapidly colder. At dusk Benny came in from watching and the three ate, talked longer, then rolled up in their blankets and went to sleep.

The Cactus Kid shivered in the cold, crisp air, his body held immobile by his bonds. He tried tensing groups of muscles to keep his circulation alive and ward off the worst of the cold, and after a while he tried his bonds. The four inches of chest expansion had given him a little slack with which to work, and he could turn his body on the dead tree. Yet for all his straining he could do little with the rawhide thongs that bound his hands behind him.

Morning dawned cold and crisp and Benny walked over to him and untied him. ''Set and eat,'' he said briefly.

For an hour they questioned him about the route south, and his answers evidently satisfied them. Much of this country was as strange to him as to them, but he did know that trail out, and he was sure that once they were traveling, his chance would come. Anyway, it was a reprieve, if only for a few days.

After having him collect more wood while watched by Joe with a rifle, they tied him again, and this time left him sitting on the ground. This time, too, he held his breath and bulged his muscles while straining for slack. And again he got it, although not so much as before.

Red was the first guard and he walked away from camp right away. Benny returned to the Kid and plied him with questions about the trail. He seemed disturbed by the trip, but why, the Cactus Kid could not gather.

Then, almost at noon, Red came in leading the horses. "We'll go," he said. "Nobody's coming. Far's a man can see, that trail's empty. We've lost 'em, but to go out thataway would be asking for trouble. The Kid can guide us over this south trail."

Although his weapons were carried by Joe Herring, the Cactus Kid was left unbound. At once, he headed off south through the mountains with Red beside him and the other Herrings immediately behind. Leaving the hills, they descended to Sage Plain, skirted Elk Ridge and the Bear's Ears, dropped into Cottonwood Wash and proceeded along it and then out into a fantastic world of eerie towers and spires like the images of cathedrals cast in stone.

At dark, he brought them up to a spring, a small trickle of water running from a fracture in the rock into a small basin, which overflowed in turn to be lost in the sand. Nearby were several windbreaks made by Indians from pine boughs or slabs of rock. There was no evidence of human life other than that, and no sign that anybody had been near in months.

Once, on the rim of a canyon, Red Herring drew up sharply.

"Thought you said there was nobody down thisaway?"

"What do you see?" the Kid asked curiously.

"House, or building over yonder." Herring stood in his stirrups and squinted. "Sort of tower."

"Oh, that?" The Kid shrugged. "Injun ruins. Lots of them down here." He turned the piebald down a steep trail to the canyon bottom. Here, in this well-watered place, they rode into groves of fir, pine, and black balsam, while snowberry and manzanita grew thick along the canyon walls. There was grass, and yet here

64

and there clumps of desert plants had invaded this richer, moister soil.

Late in the afternoon Red Herring suddenly snapped his rifle to his shoulder. Its report bellowed against the canyon walls and a mule deer plunged to its knees, tried to get up, then sprawled out.

"Nothing like fresh meat," Red said with satisfaction.

"Who skins it?" Joe demanded belligerently. "Why don't we make this sprout work?" He grinned at the Kid. "Let him earn his keep."

"Good idea," Red said, "you're cook from here on, Kid."

"Good!" the Cactus Kid said. "Now I can get some decent chuck for a while. That Joe cooks like he was fixing food for hogs."

Joe glared, and Benny chuckled. "Danged if it ain't the truth!" he said. "He had you there, Joe!"

Accepting the knife tossed to him, the Kid got busy over the deer, cutting out some fine steaks. As he worked, he was thinking swiftly. This might be the gamble he wanted, and in any event, it was worth taking a chance. As he gathered fuel for the fire and started his broiling of the steaks, he thought rapidly.

Back along the line there had been some desert brush, among them a plant he had recognized. It was a low-growing shrub, without leaves at this time of year, but with its stems dotted with odd, glandlike swellings. As he worked, the Kid kept his eyes busy and finally located the plant he sought, a relative of the rue known in many lands for medicinal effects. Carefully, from under the plant he gathered some of the dried leaves and, when making coffee, crushed a double handful and dropped them into the boiling water with the coffee. Finding more of the plants, he gathered a stack of the leaves while collecting wood and put them down not far from the fire.

Red bit into his first piece of steak, then looked up at the Kid. "You just got yourself a few more days, podner. This is *grub!*"

Even the surly Joe agreed that the Cactus Kid could cook, but when he tasted the coffee, he stared at it.

"Tastes funny," he said, scowling.

Red picked up his cup and tried it. "Tastes good to me," he said. "It's just that your taster has been ruint by that alkali and coffee junk you put out for coffee."

The Kid added more fuel to the fire. Soon they would tie him, but how soon? He had to guess right and beat them to it. Whether his stunt would work, he did not know, but it was a gamble he had to take. The Utes had told him of the plant and its effects, that it was used by them as a sedative, and that leaves thrown on a fire provided undisturbed sleep.

He poured a liberal cup of coffee for himself, but he managed to see that his cup came only after they had been served, and from a second batch that contained none of the leaves. Getting up, the Kid threw some more brush on the fire, and with it the small mound of leaves he had gathered. They burned slowly, and the smoke grew thicker, but the aroma was not unpleasant.

Benny looked up suddenly. "Joe, you better tie him up. I'm getting sleepy."

"Me too," Red agreed. "That was a long ride, and I ate more'n usual."

Joe Herring lumbered to his feet. Crossing to the Kid he jerked his wrists behind him and tied them together, his fingers clumsy with sleep. Then he tied the Kid's feet together and walked back to his bedroll.

Red was already asleep, his blanket pulled over him. At the fire, Benny dozed, and while the Cactus Kid watched hopefully, smoke drifted across his face and the man nodded. Finally, with a glance over at the Kid, Benny got up and went to his bedroll. And then, for a long time, there was silence.

———

The Kid was working hard. His breath coming hoarsely, he struggled with the poorly tied thongs on his wrists. Unable to do much with them, he hooked the toes of his boots under a log and carefully, with much struggling, succeeded in drawing his feet out of the boots. Then he backed around to them and managed to dig their toes down into the sand so that he could rub the rawhide on the rowels of his spurs. It took him more than an hour and then the thongs dropped free and he drew his wrists from behind him. They were chafed and bloody, but free!

Sitting perfectly still, he worked his fingers to restore circulation, then removed the thongs from around his boots and put them on. Crossing to the stack of guns, he picked up his own and belted them on, then put his rifle carefully to one side and considered the situation.

The Herrings were not doped. Not, at least, to the extent that they had passed out. From what he had heard, the qualities of the plant he had used were sufficient only to induce a sound sleep, which, added to their natural drowsiness from the long day in the saddle and warm food, had been sufficient. Yet he was sure that the slightest sound of a squabble and they would awaken.

Knowing them, he knew they would come

awake fighting. They would gamble. Whether he could manage without awakening them he did not know, and his first instinct was for flight. Yet here they were, the men wanted so badly, and the reward would do a lot toward stocking a ranch as well as removing from circulation some badmen no better than mad dogs.

Red was sleeping with his guns on and his rifle beside him. Benny had been more careless, yet his weapons were close. Joe, who had been carrying the Kid's weapons, had left them all together.

Moving carefully out of camp, the Kid got the piebald and saddled him. When he was ready, in case of emergency, the Kid walked slowly back to camp. Very gently, he slipped a loop over Joe's wrists and drew it as tight as he dared. The big man was sleeping with his knees drawn up, so the Kid bound his wrists down to his knees. He was just straightening up when, lifting his eyes, he looked into the startled, staring eyes of Ben Herring!

Instantly, Ben yelled. "Red! Look out! The Kid's loose!" And at the same instant he grabbed for his gun.

"Drop it!" The Cactus Kid's gun leaped into his hand. "Drop!"

Ben's finger whitened on the trigger and the Kid's gun bellowed. It was point-blank range and a fast shot. The bullet hit the cartridges in Ben's belt and glanced, smashing his elbow. The thin man dropped his gun and grabbed his arm, while on the ground Joe thrashed around, trying to free himself.

A gun bellowed from the brush and the Kid dove for shelter among some rocks. Red had not waited to draw iron, but had leaped instantly for shelter. Now he crouched there across the fire, and the Cactus Kid knew he was in for the fight of his life.

"Quiet down, Joe," the Kid called, "or I'll put a slug in you!"

Joe ceased struggling and Ben sat there by the fire, gripping his bloody arm. "I'm out of this! You crippled me!"

"See you stay out of it!" the Kid replied shortly. Then he faded back into the deeper darkness.

He was desperately worried. The night was intensely dark, and he knew from his own moving around that a man could move easily and make no sound. The trees were not too close together, and the clumps of brush could be avoided. And Red Herring was a killer, a man with every sense alert, knowing that if captured he would hang.

Moreover, the man would be filled with hatred now, and the Kid knew he had never faced a man more dangerous, more filled with concentrated evil and malice than Red Herring.

Chapter IV
Jenny's Party

The Cactus Kid lay still, well back from the fire. He knew that every second he was out of sight of the camp was a second fraught with even greater danger, for if they realized he was gone, Ben would free Joe and he would be facing two men and possibly a third.

There was no sound. The darkness lay thick and still around him. The stars were lost above a cushion of thick cloud; there was no wind. Somewhere a stone rattled, but it was far away. The Kid began to sweat. His stomach felt hollow and he stared, straining his eyes into the darkness, fighting down his desire to move, to get away from there. Yet to move might mean death, and his best plan was not to move, but to lie still, to force Red to come to him. And he knew that Red Herring, outlaw and murderer, would do just that.

One of the horses stamped, and somewhere a grouse called into the night. The Cactus Kid shifted his gun and dried his sweaty palm on his shirt. Ever so carefully, the Kid moved, sliding his body along the ground, edging toward a clump of manzanita that would permit a view of the fire.

Ben was fighting to bind his arm, and Joe was cursing steadily, staring toward the outer circle of darkness. The Kid waited, and an hour went slowly by.

Suddenly, he stiffened with realization. While he waited, tense with watching for Red, who would be stalking him, the fire was dying!

With the fire dead, and the two men in the circle of its light freed from his watching eyes, he would lose control over the situation and at once he would become the hunted, not the hunter!

Yet he dared not call out to order them to build the fire. To speak would be to have his position riddled with bullets. Cold in the blackness, he fought for a solution, and then, suddenly, he had what seemed to be the answer.

The loot.

It lay almost halfway around the circle, on the edge of the firelight. Soon the place where it lay would be in darkness. Probably as soon as he could get to it. Lying there, forgotten in the face of more immediate problems, it could be the key to the whole show. If he could get the money, then get to his horse, he might at least save the loot. And he might succeed in drawing the Herrings into a trap. For if he had the money, they would follow him.

Slowly, inch by inch, he worked his way along the ground, circling the fire. At any instant he might come face to face with Red; at any instant they might shoot it out. And over there in the circle of trees, the fire was flickering only in a few spots now.

Then the sacks of loot were there, only a short distance from his hands. With infinite care, he reached out and lifted them one by one back into the brush. Fortunately, there was little gold, so the weight was nothing to worry about. With the sacks in his left hand he eased back and got to his feet.

He found the piebald by his white spots and moved to him. The horse sidestepped and instantly the area flamed with light! A gun bellowed and a shot plucked at his sleeve.

Red Herring, guessing he would come for the saddled horse, had waited beside a stack of dry brush covered with leaves!

The flare of the fire, the stab of the shot, and his own action were one. Flinging himself in a long dive, the Kid went, not for shelter or for the horse, but straight at the stabbing flame of the shot!

A gun roared again and he heard the slam of the shot past his ear and then he was in the brush. Red Herring sprang to his feet and triggered the gun at point-blank range, but the Kid was coming too hard, and as he fired, Herring tried to step back. A rock rolled under his foot and his shot missed, and then the Cactus Kid hit him with his pistol.

Herring staggered, then caught himself and swung wickedly with the barrel of his gun for the Kid's head, but, rolling over, the Cactus Kid smashed his body against Herring's legs and the cursing outlaw went down.

Both men came up without guns and the Cactus Kid, fighting with the madness of fear, realizing his time was short, slashed into the outlaw with both fists winging. His right caught Herring on the jaw and knocked him into a tree, and before Red could set himself, the Cactus Kid closed in, smashing left and right to the head, a smashing right to the body, and a wicked left that broke Herring's nose and showered him with blood. Herring swung, missed, and his chin blocked a wicked right with all the Kid's lean, muscular power behind it. Herring hit the sand flat on his face and the Kid dove for his gun even as Joe and Ben came plowing through the brush.

"Freeze!" The Kid's gun was on them. "Drop 'em, boys, or I'll plant all of you right here!'' He had the drop . . . and they let go their guns.

———

It was midafternoon, four days later. The town was crowded with the Saturday flux of ranchers. Suddenly, there was a startled yell, and men poured into the streets.

Down the dusty main drag came four riders. Three rode abreast, and all who saw them immediately recognized the three bloody Herrings. Joe, who rode on the right, had a huge armful of sego lilies, as did Ben, who rode on the left. Red, who rode in the middle, his horse carefully roped to the other two, carried a huge armful of western forget-me-nots and purple verbena mingled with a few bunches of lilac sunbonnets.

The town stared, then it cheered, and the Herrings glowered. Up the street they went, followed by the crowd, and halted before the Simms's home.

"Oh, Nesselrode! You're *wonderful!* You got my flowers!"

"Yeah." He dismounted stiffly and began taking the flowers from the arms of the three surly outlaws. Red's head was wrapped in a bloody bandage torn from a shirt. Ben's arm was in a sling.

"Got 'em. Better get 'em in water. They may be wilted some."

If Jenny noticed the Herrings it was not obvious. "Oh, Nesselrode! I knew you could do it! I just *knew* you could!"

Joe Herring glowered. "Huh! Nesselrode! Kotched by an hombre name of *Nesselrode!*"

The Cactus Kid turned and his eyes were deadly. "I never shot a man with his hands tied, but you mention that name again and you'll be the first!"

The sheriff came pounding up with two deputies and took the prisoners.

"Well, what do you know, Jenny!" he exclaimed. "This cowpuncher of yours caught the Herring boys!"

"The Herring boys?" She smiled prettily. "Oh, Sheriff, will you ask your wife to come over and help me decorate? I don't know whether that verbena would go better in the parlor or—"

The sheriff bit off a chew.

"You catch the three meanest outlaws west of the Rockies," he said to the Kid, "and she wants to know whether the verbena will look better in one room or t'other!" He spat. "Women! I never will get 'em figured out!"

The Cactus Kid grunted, and dug out the makings. He was unshaven and the desert dust was thick on his clothes. He was half dead from his long ride and lack of sleep.

Jenny appeared suddenly in the door. "Oh, Nesselrode? Will you help me a minute, please? Pretty please?"

The Kid looked at the sheriff, and the sheriff shrugged. "Yeah," the Kid said, low-voiced. Then he looked up. "Coming, honey!" he said.

The
Ghost Maker

Author's Note

In the early days of riding and ranching, very few of the horses were more than half broken. And likely they would start bucking the moment a cowboy swung his leg over the saddle. Consequently, he wanted that pointed toe of his boot to slip easily into the stirrup, and the high heel to prevent slipping too far.

The usual practice was to bring horses in off the range to one fellow in the outfit, usually one who was a pretty good rider, who would do what they call "break the rough string." He would saddle up these unbroken horses and ride them until they stopped pitching, and that horse was considered broken.

The animal would be left there for the next cowboy to have his own little time with him, because very few of the cowboys liked a horse that wouldn't buck. And most of them did buck in the morning, especially when it was frosty.

A thoughtful rider always took his bit to the fire and warmed it some before he put it in the horse's mouth. Or sometimes he'd get it warm by wearing it inside his shirt for a while.

Marty Mahan, tall in the saddle of his black gelding, rode in the Grand Entry Parade of the Wind River Annual Rodeo, but beside him rode fear. Tall and splendidly built, clad in silver and white, Mahan was a fine-looking rider, and the crowd, which looked down to applaud, and to whose applause he responded with a wave of his Stetson, knew he was one of the greatest riders the West had seen.

For two years he had won top honors in the Wind River show. At a dozen other rodeos he was considered, by performers as well as spectators, one of the finest all-around cowboys riding the tanbark. Yet today fear rode with him, and hatred and contempt rode beside him. The fear was in the memory of a day and a horse; the hatred was in the person of big Yannell Stoper, the hard-faced roughneck of the contests, who rode beside him in the parade.

"How does it feel, Pretty Boy?" Yannell sneered. "How does it feel to know you're through? You know what they'll say when they find out? You're yellow! Yellow, Mahan! Just as yellow as they come! That Ghost Maker will show 'em today! You mark my words!"

Mahan said nothing, his face stiff and white. There was too much truth in what Stoper was saying. He was afraid—he had always been afraid of Ghost Maker.

———

Yannell Stoper had reason to know. Three times hand running, three years before, Marty Mahan had beaten Yannell out for top money, and Stoper was not a man who took losing lightly. His animosity for Mahan developed, but he had detected no flaw in the other rider until that day at Twin Forks.

It was a small rodeo, just a fill-in for riders of the stamp of Stoper and Mahan, and neither of them had figured on much trouble. Marty had won the calf roping without even extending himself, and Stoper had taken the steer wrestling easily. Both riders had allowed the lesser names to come in for money in other events, pointing themselves at the bronc riding.

Marty Mahan had been his usual devil-may-care self until the names of the riders and their mounts were posted. Marty Mahan was posted as riding Ghost Maker.

"What a name!" he said, grinning. "I wonder who thinks them up?"

Red Blade shrugged. "This one deserves his name!" he said wryly. "You should do top money if you top off that horse! He earned his name up in Calgary!"

"Calgary?" Yannell noticed a subtle change in Mahan's voice, and had turned to watch him. "This Ghost Maker from up there?"

"Sure is!" Blade spat. "Killed a man up there two seasons ago. Mighty fine rider, too. Man by the name of Cy Drannan. Throwed him an' then tromped him to death! Caught him in his teeth, flung him down, then lit in with all four feet! He's a reg'lar devil!"

"A big zebra dun?" Marty asked. Stoper recalled afterward that it had seemed less a question than a statement.

"That's right! An' pure poison!"

Marty Mahan was taken suddenly ill and could not ride. Yannell Stoper thought that one over, and curiously he watched both Marty and the dun horse. Mahan had come out to see the bronc riding, but he seemed pale and hollow-eyed. Yannell studied him shrewdly and decided that Mahan was sick all right, sick with fear. He was afraid, deathly afraid of the big dun!

And Ghost Maker did his best to live up to his name. Bud Cameron asked for the horse when Marty could not ride. Bud was thrown, lasting scarcely two seconds on the hurricane deck of the squealing, sunfishing devil of a dun. He hit the ground in a heap and staggered to his feet. Amid the roar of the crowd, Mahan leaped up, screaming!

His voice was lost in the thunder of shouting, lost to all but Stoper, who was watching the man he hated. He saw that scream was a scream of fear, but of warning, too! For the zebra dun, neck stretched and teeth bared, knocked the puncher sprawling and lit into him with both feet. They got the maddened animal away from the fallen man, but before nightfall the word was around. Bud Cameron would never ride again. He would never walk again. He was crippled for life.

Big, tawny, lion-headed Yannell Stoper had no thought of Bud Cameron. The breaks of the game. What he did think about was Marty Mahan, for Marty was afraid. He was afraid of Ghost Maker. It was something to remember.

At Prescott and Salinas, Mahan beat Stoper out for top money, but Ghost Maker was not around. He was piling riders down in Texas and killing his second man. Stoper made sure that

Marty knew about that. After Marty won at Salinas, Yannell congratulated him.

"Lucky for you it wasn't the Ghost Maker," Yannell said. Mahan's head came up, his face gone pale. "I see he killed another man down in Texas!"

Mahan, his face white, had walked away without speaking. Behind him, Yannell had smiled grimly. This was something to know.

Yannell Stoper had his own ideas about men. A man who was afraid of anything was a man who was yellow. It was just in him, that was all. He did not know that a man who can face fists is often deathly afraid of a gun, and that a gunman may shrink from the cold steel of a knife. Or a man of utmost cowardice before some kinds of danger may face another kind with high courage. To Yannell Stoper a man who was yellow was yellow, and that was final. And to his satisfaction, Marty Mahan was yellow. It was a fact to be remembered and to be used.

Yannell Stoper was big, rugged, and rough. In a lifetime of battling with hard broncs and harder men he had rarely known defeat, and never known fear. He had nothing but contempt for men who were afraid of anything, or who admitted doubt of themselves in any situation that demanded physical courage.

Now, on this day at the Wind River Rodeo, Yannell Stoper was ready for his triumph. It was a triumph that would mean much to him, one he had carefully engineered. For it was at Stoper's suggestion that the contest officials had secured the string of rough buckers of which the Ghost Maker was one.

Here in Wind River, before the world of the rodeo and the eyes of Peg Graham he would expose the cowardice of Marty Mahan for all the world to see.

"He's here!" Yannell taunted. "Right here in Wind River, an' if you duck ridin' him here they'll all know you're yellow!"

———

They would, too! Even Marty had heard, or rather, overheard, the stories. He knew Stoper had started them himself, planting the seeds for the exposure, removing at once his rival for top rodeo honors and for Peg Graham.

"They say Mahan will drop out rather than ride Ghost Maker," a big rancher had said the evening before. "He's scared of the hoss! Dropped out of a show down in Texas rather than tackle him!"

"He's a bad horse," Red Carver admitted, "but you never make a good ride on an easy one!"

Marty had turned away and walked back toward the hotel, sick and ashamed. For he was afraid. He had been afraid of Ghost Maker from the day he had first seen him on that lonely Nevada range where he had run wild. He had been afraid of him ever since he had seen the dun lift his head, nostrils flared, and then come mincing toward him, walking so quietly away from the herd.

A wild horse that did not run. That should have warned him, and if it had not, the reaction of his own mount would have, for his horse began to quiver and edge away, blowing with fright. An old rancher had told Marty once, ''Kill him the second he shows he's a killer, or he'll get you sure!''

Real man-killers were rare, but there was in them something of a fiend, of a destroying demon that came on so gently, then charged with wide jaws and flaring eyes. And Ghost Maker was such a horse, a horse marked from birth with a vicious hatred of man or even of other horses, of anything that moved and was not of his own herd.

Mahan had been seventeen at the time he first glimpsed the Ghost Maker. He had felt his horse shy, felt the quivering fright in the animal. Marty was younger then and he was curious. Above all, this wild horse seemed so tame, so friendly.

Suddenly the dun had darted at them, frenzied with killing fury. In a flash he had struck down Mahan's saddle horse. Marty had fallen free and the dun had rushed at him, but the effort of his gray to get off the ground distracted the maddened horse, and the stallion had wheeled and struck wickedly at the gray. Fighting like a very fiend incarnate, the zebra dun had attacked the gray horse and struck and slashed until the saddle horse was a bloody heap of dead flesh, hammered, chopped, and pounded until all life was gone and even the saddle was a ruined and useless thing.

Marty, crouching weaponless between two boulders, watched that holocaust of butchery with horror-stricken eyes, unable to do anything to protect the old saddle horse he had ridden. And then, his killing fury unabated, the dun had come for him, lunging with slashing hoofs at the rocks, but unable because of the position in which he lay, to get at the boy.

For three fear-haunted hours the killer dun had circled those rocks. Time and again he struggled to get at the boy lying in the crevice. In those hours had been born an overwhelming horror of the horse. A horror that was never forgotten. Long after the horses had gone, led away by the dun on some whim of the wild, Marty had lain there, cramped and still, fearing to move, fearing to show himself in the open where the stallion might again come upon him.

Never again had he gone up on the range without a pistol, but never again had he gone to that section of the range. He had seen no more of the horse until that day in Calgary when the dun had shown itself under the saddle of Cy Drannan, Marty's best friend. Marty had hurried to the rider and told him the horse was a killer.

"So what?" Drannan shrugged. "I've heard of killers but never seen one! I always figured I'd like to top one off!"

Cy Drannan, happy, friendly, a good companion and rider, died on the bloody tanbark that day under the lashing hoofs of a horse that was a cunning, hate-ridden devil.

Now that horse was here, in this show, and *he* was to ride him. He, Marty Mahan.

———

Peg Graham was waiting for him when the parade ended. Her eyes were bright.

"Oh, Marty! Dad's said that after the rodeo if you will buy that Willow Creek range he will give his consent!"

Marty nodded soberly. "Does it have to be right away, honey?" he asked. "I mean, I . . . well, I may not make enough money in this show. Added to what I have, it will have to be a good fifteen hundred to swing that deal. I'd have to win four events to make it.''

''Not if you win the bronc riding, Marty! They've upped the prize money and have offered a flat thousand dollars for top money! You can win it! You've already beaten both Red Carver and Yannell Stoper before!''

He hesitated, his face flushing. ''I'm not riding broncs in this show, Peg,'' he said slowly. ''I'm going to go in for calf roping, bull riding, steer wrestling, and some other stuff, but not bronc riding.''

Peg Graham's face had turned a shade whiter, and her eyes widened. ''Then . . . then it's true what they say! You are afraid!''

He looked at her, then glanced away, his heart miserable within him. ''Yeah, I guess I am,'' he said, ''I guess I am afraid of that horse!''

Peg Graham stared at him, ''Marty, I'll never marry a coward! I'll never have it said that my man was afraid to ride a horse that other men would ride! Red Carver has asked for that horse! Yannell says—''

''Yannell?'' Marty looked at the girl. ''You've been talking to him?''

''Yes, I have!'' she flashed. ''At least, he's not afraid of a horse!'' She turned on her heel and walked swiftly away, every inch of her quivering with indignation.

Mahan started to turn, then stopped. An old man with a drooping yellowed mustache leaned against the corral.

"Tough, kid!" he said. "I didn't aim to overhear, but couldn't help it. You up to ride the Ghost Maker?"

Marty nodded. "I'm not ridin' him, though!" he said. "That horse is a devil! He shouldn't be allowed in shows like this! That isn't sport or skill. . . . It's plain, unadulterated murder!"

"Reckon I agree with you," the old-timer said seriously. "It ain't a bit smart to tackle a horse like that! I've seen him in action, an' he's a killer all through!"

Marty nodded unhappily. "He's from my home range in the Black Rock Desert country. He killed my ridin' horse once, about five years ago."

"You Marty Mahan?" the old man inquired. "I'm Old John. Heard a lot about you. You don't look like no coward."

Marty's eyes flashed. "I'm not! But I am afraid of that horse! I'm not aimin' to fool anybody about that!"

"Takes a good man to admit he's scared," Old John commented thoughtfully. "Who rides him if you don't?"

"Carver an' Stoper both want him. I wish they'd leave him out of this. He's a killer and a devil. There's something in that horse that ain't right."

"Like some men I know," John agreed. "There's killers in all sorts of critters. Just got a streak of meanness an' devil in 'em." He hitched up his pants. "Well, luck to you, son. I'll be amblin'."

Marty Mahan stared after the old man, his brow furrowed. He had never seen *him* around before.

The memory of Peg's face cut him like a knife. She believed him a coward. . . . Well, maybe he was! He walked over to Jeff Allen, chairman of the rodeo committee.

"Jeff, I'm withdrawin' from the bronc ridin'. I won't ride that Ghost Maker."

Allen shifted his cigar in his jaws. "Heard you didn't aim to. You say he's a killer?"

"He sure is." Briefly, Marty related his own experiences with the horse. "Personally, I think you should take him out of the lists."

Jeff Allen shook his head. His cold blue eyes showed disdain. "Not a chance! Just because you're afraid to tackle him don't mean others won't! Stoper has been around here, beggin' for him!"

Marty saw nothing of Peg Graham, nor of her father. Alone, he waited by the chutes for the calf roping, which was the first event in which he was entered. None of the rodeo hands stopped near him, nor did the contestants. Bitterly, his heart heavy in his chest, he watched them and watched the crowd. Once, over beyond the corral he saw Peg Graham. She was with Yannell Stoper.

Stoper opened in the calf roping and made a quick chase, a clean catch, and a fast tie. It was good time. Red Carver and Bent Wells fell a little short. Marty Mahan's black was a darting flash when the calf left the pens. He swept down his rope streaking like a thrown lance. The catch was perfect and he hit the ground almost as the rope tightened. He dropped his calf, made his tie, and straightened to his feet, his hands in the air.

"Folks!" Roberts boomed. "That's mighty fast time! Marty Mahan, internationally famous rodeo star, makes his tie in eleven and two-tenths seconds!"

Three-tenths of a second better than Stoper. Marty turned, amid cheers, toward his black horse, and then somebody—and away down within him, Marty was sure it was Stoper—yelled:

"Where's the Ghost Maker? Get Ghost Maker!"

The crowd took it up, and as Marty cantered from the arena his ears rang with the taunting word.

"Get Ghost Maker! Let him ride Ghost Maker! *Yellow!*"

White-faced, he dropped to the ground. Old John looked up at him.

"Hard to take, ain't it, boy?"

Mahan did not reply, but his face was pale and set. Yannell Stoper came around the corral, several riders with him.

"There's the hero! Wants milk-wagon horses!"

Marty turned sharply. "That will be enough of that!" he snapped.

Yannell halted, astonished. Then his eyes narrowed. "Why, you yeller-bellied, white-livered son—!"

They started for each other, fists clenched. The loudspeaker boomed out.

"Stoper! Ready for steer wrestling! Stoper! On your horse!"

With a curse the big tawny-headed man turned. "Saved you from a beatin'!" he sneered. "You get the breaks!"

"See me later, then!" Marty flashed back at him. "Anywhere! Any time!"

Grimly, he walked away. Behind him he heard the roar of the crowd as Yannell went after his steer. For a minute Marty Mahan stood still, listening to that roar behind him. Soon he would be going out there, facing that crowd again, and they would taunt and boo again. It was no use. . . . Why bother? He might as well quit now!

Then another thought came and he stopped in midstride. Run? Like the devil he would! He'd go back there and make them eat their taunts. Every word! He wheeled and walked back. When the time came for him to go out he went like a demon, flashing with speed. He took his steer down faster than ever before in his life, and as the loudspeaker boomed out his time, he swung into the saddle.

Taunts and jeers burst from the stands, but this time instead of riding out, he rode over before the stands and sat there, his hat lifted in salute. As the yells, boos, and hisses swept the arena, he sat perfectly still, his face dead-white, his eyes bright, waiting for stillness. It came at last. Then he waved his hat once more and, turning his horse, walked him quietly from the arena, leaving dead silence behind him.

Old John stood beside Peg Graham, who watched, her eyes wide. "That," Old John commented dryly, "took sand!"

She turned quickly to look at him. Then her eyes went back to the man riding from the arena. "I . . . guess it did," she agreed hesitantly.

Her brows puckered. "I don't know you, do I?"

Old John rolled his quid in his jaws. "No, ma'am, you don't. Nor a real man when you see him!" He turned abruptly and walked off, leaving the girl's face flushing with embarrassment and shame.

As she turned away, she wondered. Had she wronged Marty Mahan? Was he a coward because he refused to ride that horse? If a man went into contest riding, he was not expected to be afraid of bad horses. He was expected to ride anything given him. Mostly the riders wanted bad horses because it gave them the best chance to make a good ride. Even if this horse was as bad as Mahan claimed, was it reason for refusing?

In the last analysis, she guessed it was simply that she could not bear to have him called a coward, or to love a man who was yellow.

Yannell Stoper won the bareback bronc riding in both the first and second go-rounds. Then he appeared in his usual exhibition of trick riding, and the first day of the rodeo ended with Stoper as the hero of the show despite his loss to Marty in the calf roping. His insistence on riding the horse that Mahan refused caught the crowd's interest.

Mahan was disconsolate. He walked the

streets, feeling singularly out of place in his expensive trappings, and wishing he were miles away. Only the knowledge that if he left the show he would be branded a quitter, and through in the arena, kept him in town. That and the fascination exerted over him by the dun horse.

As the evening drew on he heard more and more talk of the dun. Despite their willingness to call him a coward for refusing the horse, people were beginning to wonder if the animal were not a killer after all. At all these rumors Yannell scoffed.

Marty Mahan was at supper when the café door slammed open and big, tawny-haired Stoper came in with Red Carver and Peg Graham. When the girl saw Marty sitting at the table alone she would have turned to leave, but Yannell would have none of it. They trooped in and, with several hangers-on, seated themselves at tables near Mahan's. At the counter not far away sat Old John, calmly eating doughnuts and drinking coffee.

"Sure I'll ride him!" Stoper boomed loudly. "I'm not yellow! I'll ride anything that wears hair!"

Mahan looked up. Inside he was strangely still and at ease. It was only his mind that seemed suddenly white-hot, yet his eyes were clear and hard. He looked across at Yannell Stoper and their eyes met.

"Finally got showed up, didn't you?" Stoper sneered. "You was always a four-flusher!"

"And you were always a loudmouth," Marty said quietly.

Stoper's face flushed red. Then his blue-white eyes narrowed down and he began to smile. He pushed back from the table.

"I always wanted to get my hands on you and in just about a minute I'll slap all the coward to the surface!"

He got up and started around the table. Carver called to him, and Peg Graham got up, her hand going to her mouth, eyes wide and frightened.

"And in just about a half minute," Marty said, sliding out of his chair, "you'll wish you'd never opened your mouth!"

Stoper walked in smiling and when he got to arm's length, he swung. It was a powerful, wide-armed punch, but Mahan's left shot straight from the shoulder to Stoper's mouth, setting the big rider back on his heels. Then Marty crossed with a smashing right that dropped Yannell to his haunches.

Mahan stepped back, his face calm. "If you want to ride that horse tomorrow," he said, "you'd better save it!"

Stoper came up with a lunge and dove for Marty, who stepped into a chair and tripped. Before he could regain his balance, Stoper was on him with a smashing volley of punches. Mahan staggered and Yannell was all over him, his face set in a mask of fury, his punches smashing and driving. Yet somehow Mahan weathered the storm, covered and got in close. Grabbing Yannell by the belt with one hand and a knee with the other, he upended the furious puncher and dropped him to the floor.

Stoper came up with a growl of rage and Mahan smashed a left and right to the face. The left went to the mouth, to Stoper's already bleeding lips, and showered him with blood. Marty stepped to the side and avoided a right, then countered with a wicked right to the wind. Yannell gasped and Mahan stabbed a left, then hooked hard to the face. Stoper bulled in close and the two men stood toe to toe amid the wreckage of smashed crockery and threw punches with both hands.

Both men were big and both were powerful. Stoper weighed well over two hundred and Mahan scaled close to the one-ninety mark. Both were in excellent shape. Stoper roared in close and grabbed Marty. They went to the floor. Stabbing at Mahan's eyes with his thumbs, Stoper missed and fell forward just as Marty smashed upward with his head. Blinded by pain, Stoper was thrown off, and then Marty lunged to his feet. Stoper got up, blinking away the tears the smash had brought to his eyes. Mahan measured him with a left, then hooked right and left to the body. Yannell shook his mane of tawny hair and swung a powerful, freckled fist. It missed, and Marty hit him again in the middle. The big rider stooped and Mahan slugged him twice more and the big man wilted and went to the floor.

"Who's yellow, Yannell?" Marty said then. He mopped the sweat from his brow with a quick motion of his hand and stepped back. "Get up if you want more. You can have it."

"I'll get up!" Stoper gasped, and heaved himself erect.

Mahan stared at the swaying, punch-drunk rider. Stoper's eyes were glazed; blood dripped from his smashed lips and from a long cut over his eye. A blue mouse was rising under the other eye. His ear was bleeding. Marty stepped back and dropped his hands.

"You're no fighter," he said dryly, "an' too good a rider to beat to death!" He turned abruptly and walked out of the café.

Yannell Stoper brushed a hand dazedly across his eyes and stared after him in drunken concentration, trying to make sense of a man who would walk away from a helpless enemy. He shook his big head and, turning, staggered blindly to a chair at a vacant table. He slumped into it and rested his head on his arms.

———

The second day of the rodeo was a study in delay. Despite his beating of the night before, Yannell Stoper looked good. His face was raw and battered, but physically he seemed in good shape and he was fast and smooth. Marty Mahan, working to absolute silence from the crowd, won the finals in the calf tying by bettering his previous time by a tenth of a second. Stoper was second.

Stoper won the steer wrestling, and took the finals in the bareback bucking contest.

Marty came out on Old Seven-Seventy-Seven, a big and vicious Brahma bull who knew all the tricks. The bull weighed a shade more than a ton and had never had a stiff battle. He came out full of fight, bucking like a demon, swiveling his hips, hooking left and right with his short, blunted horns, fighting like mad to unseat the rider who clung to the rigging behind his hump. Marty was going and he was writing over both flanks, giving the big Brahma all the metal he could stand.

Old Seven went into a wicked spin, then

suddenly reversed. The crowd gasped, expecting the speed of it to unseat Mahan, but when the dust cleared, Marty was still up there, giving the bull a spur-whipping he would never forget. The whistle blew and Mahan unloaded with a dive. But Old Seven wasn't through by a whole lot. He wheeled like a cat on a hot stove and came for Marty full tilt. Mahan swung around, and then the clowns dove in and one of them flicked the big bull across the nose and the maddened animal came around and went for the clown. Marty walked off the tanbark to the scattered cheers of the crowd.

"Quiet today, Marty," Carver said, hesitantly.

Mahan looked up, a queer half-smile on his face. "They are waiting, Red. They want to see the Ghost Maker."

"Stoper's riding him. I lost out."

"You're lucky," Mahan said dryly. "That's no ordinary bad horse, Red. Take it from me."

Suddenly he saw Jeff Allen before him and he turned abruptly and walked toward him.

"Jeff," he said abruptly, "I want to be in the arena when Stoper rides Ghost Maker."

The older man hesitated, looking coldly at Mahan. "You had your chance to ride him," he said briefly. "Now let Stoper do it."

"I aim to," Mahan replied. "However, I don't want to see him killed!"

Allen jerked his head impatiently. "You leave that to Stoper. He ain't yellow!"

"Am I?" Marty asked quietly.

For a moment the eyes of the two men held. The hard-bitten oldster was suddenly conscious that he was wearing a gun. It was only part of the rodeo trappings, but it was loaded, and so was the gun on Mahan's hip. The days of gunfighting were past, and yet . . . Marty's eyes met his, cold and bleak.

"Why, I don't reckon you are," Jeff said suddenly. "It just seemed sort of funny, you backin' out on that horse, that's all!"

Mahan looked at him with hard eyes. "The next time something seems funny to you, Jeff, you just laugh! Hear me? Don't insinuate a man is yellow. Just laugh!" He turned on his heel and walked away.

Dick Graham looked after him thoughtfully, then said, "Jeff, I thought for a minute you were goin' to fill that long-time vacant space up in Boot Hill!"

Allen swallowed and mopped the sweat from his face. "Darned if I didn't myself!" he said, relieved. "That hombre would have drawed iron!"

"You're not just a-woofin'!" Graham said dryly. "That boy may be a lot of things, but he isn't yellow! Look what he did to Yannell last night!''

———

Yannell Stoper walked down to Chute Five. The Ghost Maker, a strapping big zebra dun, stood quietly waiting in the chute. He was saddled and bridled, and he made no fuss awaiting the saddle, having taken the bit calmly. Now he knew what was coming, and he waited, knowing his time was soon. Deep within his equine heart and mind something was twisted and hot, something with a slow fuse that was burning down, close to the dynamite within him.

At one side of the arena, white-faced and ready, astride his black roping horse, sat Marty Mahan. Time and again eyes strayed to him wonderingly, and one pair of those eyes belonged to Peg Graham. Yannell, despite himself, was nervous. He climbed up on the chute, waved a gloved hand, and settled in the saddle. He felt the horse bunch his muscles, then relax.

"All right," Stoper said. Then he yelled, "Cut her loose!" And then the lid blew off.

Ghost Maker left the chute with a lunge, sandwiched his head between his forelegs, and went to bucking like a horse gone mad. He was leaving the ground thirty inches at each jump and exploding with such force that blood gushed from Yannell's mouth with his third jump.

He buck-jumped wickedly in a tight circle, and then, when Yannell's head was spinning like a top, the maddened horse began to swap ends with such speed that he was almost a blur. Caught up in the insane rhythm of the pounding hoofs, Yannell was betrayed by a sudden change as the horse sprang sideways. He left the saddle and hit the ground, jarred in every vertebra.

Drunken with the pounding he had taken, he lunged to his feet, to see the horse charging him, eyes white and glaring, teeth bared. The crowd came off its seats in one long scream of horror as the maddened horse charged down on the dazed and helpless rider.

In some blind half-awareness of danger, Yannell stumbled aside. At the instant, Mahan's black horse swept down upon the maddened beast and Mahan's rope darted for the killer's head. Distracted, Ghost Maker jerked and the throw missed. Like an avenging demon he hurled himself at Marty's black, ripping a gash in the black horse's neck. The black wheeled, and the crowd screamed in horror as they saw him stumble and go down.

Out of the welter of dust and confusion somebody yelled, "Marty's up! Marty's on him!"

In the nightmare of confusion as the black fell, Marty, cold with fear of the maddened horse, grabbed out wildly and got one hand on the saddle horn of Ghost Maker. With every ounce of strength he had, he scrambled for the saddle and made it!

Out of the dust the screaming, raging horse lunged, bucking like mad, a new rider in the saddle. In some wild break of fortune, Mahan had landed with his feet in the stirrups, and now as Yannell crawled away, blood streaming from his nose, and the black threshed on the ground, Marty was up in the middle of the one horse on earth that he feared and hated.

Ghost Maker, with a bag full of tricks born in his own hate-filled brain, began to circle-buck in the same vicious tight circle that had taken Stoper from the saddle. At the height of his gyrations he suddenly began to swap ends in a blur of speed. Mahan, frightened and angry, suddenly exploded into his own private fury and began to pour steel to the horse. Across the arena they went while riders stood riveted in amazement, with Marty Mahan writing hiero-glyphics all over the killer's flanks with both spurs.

Pitching like a fiend, Ghost Maker switched to straightaway bucking mingled with snakelike contortions of his spine, tightening and uncoiling like a steel spring.

Riders started cutting in from both sides, but Marty was furious now.

"Stay away!" he roared. "I'll ride him to a finish or kill him!"

And then began such a duel between horse and man as the rodeo arena at Wind River had never seen. The horse was a bundle of hate-filled energy, but the rider atop him was remembering all those long years down from his lost riding horse on the desert, and he was determined to stay with the job he had shunned. Riders circled warily out of reach, but now long after any ten-second whistle would have blown, Marty was up on the hurricane deck of the killer and whipping him to a frazzle. The horse dropped from his bucking and began to trot placidly across the arena, and then suddenly he lunged like a shot from a cannon, straight for the wall of the stands.

People screamed and sprang away as if afraid the horse might actually bound into the stands, but he wheeled and hurled his side against the board wall with force that would have crushed Marty's leg instantly. Mahan, cool and alert now, kicked his foot free and jerked the leg out of the way the instant before the horse hit.

As the animal bounded away, injured by its

own mad dive, Mahan kicked his toe back into the stirrup and again began to feed steel to the tiring killer. But now the horse had had enough. Broken in spirit, he humped his back and refused to budge. For an instant Marty sat there, and then he dropped from the beaten horse to the ground and his legs almost gave way under him.

He straightened, and the killer, in one last burst of spirit, lunged at him, jaws agape. Standing his ground, Marty smashed the horse three times across the nose with his hat, and the animal backed up, thoroughly cowed.

Taking the bridle, Marty started back toward the chute, leading the beaten horse and trembling in every limb. Behind him, docile at last, walked Ghost Maker.

The emotion-wracked crowd stared at this new spectacle, and then suddenly someone started to cheer, and they were still cheering and cheering when Marty Mahan stopped by the corral and passed the bridle of the horse to a rider. He turned and leaned against the corral, still trembling. For the first time he realized that his nose was bleeding and that the front of his white rodeo costume was red with spattered blood.

Yannell Stoper, his own clothing bloody, walked up to him, hand out.

"Marty," he said sincerely, "I want to apologize. You sure ain't yella, an' you sure saved my bacon! An' that was the greatest ride a man ever made!"

"You sure weren't afraid of that horse!" Dick Graham said. "Why, man . . . !"

"Afraid of him?" Marty looked up grimly. "You're durned right I was afraid of him! I was never so scared in my life! I didn't get on that horse because I *wanted* to! It was the safest place there was! An' once up there, I sure enough had to stay on or be killed! Scared? Mister, I was never so scared in my life!"

Old John was standing nearby grinning at him. "Nice goin', boy. An' by the way, I heard you an' the lady here"—he indicated Peg Graham—"were interested in my Willow Creek ranch outfit. If you still are, I would sell it mighty cheap, to the right couple!"

Peg was looking at him, wide-eyed and pale. "I . . . I don't know if . . . ?" Her voice was doubtful.

Marty straightened and slid an arm around her. "Sure thing, John! Looks like it would be a nice place to raise horses an' . . ."

"Cattle?" Red Carver asked, grinning.

"Kids!" Marty said. "Lots of kids! All rodeo riders!" He looked at Peg, grinning. "Okay?"

"Okay," she agreed.

The Drift

Author's Note

In the old days it was very common to see a cowboy with one or two fingers missing. Most likely there was a bad steer on the other end of the rope he had dallied around his saddle horn. His hand would get caught and a finger might get cut off or pulled off. So in every group of seven or eight cowboys you'd find one or two who had a finger gone.

Smoke Lamson came into the bunkhouse and Johnny Garrett cringed. The big foreman rolled his tobacco in his jaws and looked slowly around the room.

Nobody looked up. Nobody said anything. It was a wicked night, blowing snow and cold, so it was a foregone conclusion who was going to night-herd.

"You"—he turned suddenly to Johnny—"saddle up and get out there. An' remember, if they start to drift, make 'em circle."

Johnny swung his feet to the floor. "Why me?" he protested. "I've been on night ridin' every night this week."

Lamson grinned. "Good for you, kid. Make a man out of you. Get goin'."

An instant, Johnny Garrett hesitated. He could always quit. He could draw his time. But how long would forty dollars last? And where else could he get a job at this time of the year?

117

More-over, if he left the country he would never see Mary Jane again.

He drew on his boots, then his chaps and sheepskin. He pulled the rawhide under his chin and started for the door.

Lasker rolled over on his bunk. "Kid, you can take my Baldy if you want. He's a good night horse."

"Thanks," Johnny said. "I'll stick to my string. They might as well learn."

"Sure." Smoke Lamson grinned and started to build a smoke. "Like you, they gotta learn."

Johnny opened the door, the lamp guttered, and then he was outside, bending his head into the wind. By now he should be used to it.

———

He had come to the Bar X from Oregon, where he had grown up in the big timber, but he came to Arizona wanting to punch cows. After a couple of short jobs he had stumbled into the Bar X when they needed a hand. The boss hired him, and Lamson did not like that, but he had said nothing, done nothing until that night in town.

Everybody on the Bar X knew that Smoke was sweet on Mary Jane Calkins. Everybody, that is, but Johnny Garrett. And Johnny had seen Mary Jane, danced with her, talked with her, and then walked out with her. Looking for Mary Jane, Smoke had found them in a swing together.

He had been coldly furious, and Mary Jane, apparently unaware of what she was doing, told Smoke that Johnny was going to be a top hand by spring. "You wait an' see," Johnny had said.

And Smoke Lamson looked at Johnny and grinned slowly. "You know, Mary Jane," he said meaningfully, "I'll bet he is!"

That started it. Every tough and lonely job fell to Johnny Garrett. Morning, noon, and night he was on call. Everybody in the bunkhouse could see that Smoke was riding Johnny, driving him, trying to make him quit. "Want to be a top hand, don't you?" he would taunt. "Get on out there!" And Johnny went.

He mended what seemed to be miles of fence, and if Lamson did not think it was well done, it was done over. He cut wood for the cook, the lowest of cow ranch jobs; he hunted strays in the wildest and roughest country; he used a shovel more than a rope, cleaning water holes, opening springs. He did more night riding than any three men in the outfit. He worked twelve and fourteen hours a day when the others rarely did more than seven or eight in the fall and bitter winter.

Smoke Lamson was big and he was tough. It was his boast that he had never been bested in a rough-and-tumble fight, and although he outweighed Johnny by forty pounds, he seemed to be trying to tempt the smaller man to try his luck.

As the months went by it grew worse. As if angered by his failure to force Johnny to quit, Lamson became tougher. Even Lasker, a taciturn man, attempted to reason with Smoke. "Why don't you lay off the kid?" he demanded. "He's doin' his job."

"My business, Dan." Smoke was abrupt. "When he's as good a hand as you or me, I'll lay off."

———

Johnny got the saddle on his dun and rode out of the big barn, ducking his head under the door. From the saddle he swung the door shut, then turned the horse into the wind and headed toward the west range.

Ice was already forming and the ground had white patches of snow, but there was more in the air, blowing as well as falling, than on the ground. It was blowing cold and bitter from the north, and if the cattle started to drift and got any kind of a start, there would be no stopping them. Not far below the valley where he would be riding was Sage Flat, fifty miles wide and half again that long, and nothing to stop them in all that length but a forty-foot arroyo. If they started south ahead of the wind, they would be half-frozen by the time they reached that arroyo and would walk off into it.

Johnny had heard about a drift. He had never seen it, but his imagination was good.

He had been in the saddle over an hour when he saw the first steer, a big roan steer, heading toward him, plodding steadily. Behind him there was another, then another . . . and for the first time, he knew panic.

Deep inside he knew that nobody had ever expected this. The upper end of the valley he patrolled was fenced, and Smoke had sent him here just for safety's sake or out of pure cussedness, but the fence must be down, must have been pushed over, and they were coming.

There was no time to go for help. He drew his pistol and fired into the air, partly hoping to stop the drift, partly to call for help. It did neither. Desperately, he tried to turn the cattle, and they would not turn. When he got one half-turned into the storm, others would go by him.

And from up the valley came more, and more, and more.

Then he realized the full enormity of what

was happening. The whole herd, more than a thousand head, would be drifting ahead of the norther. Unless stopped they would drift into the arroyo, winding up at the bottom either dead or with broken legs, helpless, for the cold to kill. A few would survive, of course, but not many. A forty-foot fall into a rocky ravine is not calculated to do either man or animal any good.

The dun worked hard. Johnny yelled, fired more shots, tried everything. The cattle kept coming. He had forgotten Smoke Lamson, who had sent him here. He had forgotten everything but the cattle and the kindly old man, old Bart Gavin, who had hired him when he was broke.

He drew up, staring into the storm. Ice was forming on the scarf over his chin. His toes were numb from inactivity, and the cattle drifted. It was four miles to the gate, four more to the bunkhouse. To go there and get back with the hands—for they must all dress and saddle up— would let too many cattle go by. And what could be done when they got here?

By daybreak a thousand head of beef steers would be piled up along a mile or so of that arroyo. Unless . . . unless he could force them over. If he could push them east to the flank of Comb Ridge, start them down along the ridge until they got between the ridge and Gavin

Fault, he might force them to pile up in one place. Some would be lost but the fall of the others would be cushioned. . . . An idea clicked in his mind.

Swinging the startled dun, he slammed the spurs to the mustang and raced south. He passed steer after steer, plodding steadily, methodically on, hypnotized by their movement and driven by the howling norther behind them. Racing on at breakneck speed over the frozen ground, he was soon beyond them. As he raced, he was thinking. They were traveling slow, the usual slow walk of a drift herd. There would be, with luck, time enough.

Soon he was passing the straggling leaders, strung out for a quarter of a mile, and then he was racing alone into the night and the south, away from the herd, toward the arroyo. Yet, when a few miles were behind him he swung off west and rode hard. Suddenly he saw a shoulder of Gavin Fault, a huge upthrust of sandstone. Keeping it close on his left, he rode down it until against the night he caught the square shoulder of Rock House. He swung the dun into the lee of the house and got out of the saddle.

The door opened when he lifted the latch and shoved. He got in quickly and struck a match. Against the wall were piled four boxes of powder. He stuffed it into sacks, caught up a roll of fuse, and ran from the shack, closing the door after him.

Putting the giant powder behind the saddle, he got up himself, and, the fuses around his arm, heedless of risk, he rode on south. If the dun stumbled and fell—well, there would be a mighty big hole in the grass!

The dun liked to run, and it was bitter cold now. How cold he did not know, but getting down there. He raced onward until suddenly he saw ahead of him the black line of the arroyo. He swung from the dun and led the horse into the shelter of a rocky projection and hurried to the edge. Carefully, he clambered down.

He knew that spot. He had slipped away and hidden from Lamson to catch a quiet smoke on several occasions. It was cracked and honeycombed with holes. Working swiftly, he stuffed the cracks with powder, jammed bunches of sticks into holes, and worked his way from the lip almost to the bottom. He had been working for more than a half hour before he saw the first steer. It had brought up against a rock some distance off and stood there, befuddled. It would soon come on.

Sheltered from the wind that blew over the lip above him, Johnny ran along, hastily spitting his fuses. When all were lighted that he could see, he scrambled back up and grabbed his horse. He was riding into the teeth of the wind when he heard the blast. There was no time to go back. It had to work. It must work.

North he rode until he saw the cattle. They were coming now in droves, and soon he was past the end of the fault. Channeled by the valley from which they had come, the animals plodded steadily ahead. Only a few seemed inclined to stray west, and these he pushed back. He could move them east or west, but no power on earth could now prevent them from going south.

How long he worked he did not know. Every move might be futile. Once the dun fell, but scrambled gamely up. Soon Johnny found a place from which he could watch for some distance. The snow was letting up, the ground was white, and visibility not bad. He worked more slowly, half-dead in the saddle, and then the last of the cattle drifted by and he turned his horse and walked slowly back to the ranch.

Half-dead with weariness, he stripped the saddle from his horse and then went to work. For half an hour he worked hard over the dun, and then he blanketed the horse to allow him to conserve as much heat as possible. Stumbling, he got into the bunkhouse and crawled into bed. His feet were numbed and for a while he held his toes, trying to warm them. And then he fell asleep.

A hand on his shoulder awakened him. It was Dan Lasker. "Better crawl out, kid. Lamson's on a tear this mornin'."

He was the last one to reach the breakfast table. He came into the room and stopped abruptly. Sitting with Bart Gavin was a girl . . . and what a girl!

Her hair was dark and thick, her eyes bright, her lips slightly full and red. In a daze he got into a chair and hitched close to the table. The hands were tongue-tied. No conversation this morning. In front of the radiant creature beside Bart they were completely at a loss. Even Smoke Lamson was speechless.

Suddenly, she spoke. "Why is it that only one of the horses has a blanket on him? It was so cold last night!"

"Blanket?" Gavin looked around. "Blanket on a horse?"

The hands looked around, astonished. The tough Western cow ponies were unaccustomed to such treatment. Even Smoke Lamson was surprised. Suddenly he turned on Johnny, seeing a chance to have some fun. "Maybe it was the Top Hand here. That sounds like him."

The dark and lovely eyes turned to Johnny and he blushed furiously.

"Did oo w'ap up the po' itto hossie?" Lamson said, glancing at the girl to see if his wit was appreciated, and chuckling.

Gavin looked at Johnny sharply. Feeling some explanation necessary, Johnny said feebly, "He was pretty wore out. It was near to daybreak before I got in."

Gavin put his fork down. "Daybreak?" He was incredulous. "What were you doing out last night?"

It was Lamson's turn to grow confused. He hesitated. Then he said, "I figured somebody better watch in case of a drift."

"A *drift?*" Gavin's voice was scornful. "With that fence? It's horse high and bull strong! Anyway"—his voice was biting—"what could one man do against a drift?"

Smoke Lamson stuttered, hesitated, and finally tried a feeble excuse. The girl looked from him to Johnny, and then at the other hands. Bart Gavin was no fool. He was beginning to realize something he had not realized before.

"The cows are all right." Johnny found a voice. "I was there when the drift started. They are in the arroyo."

"*What?*" Bart Gavin came out of his seat, his face shocked and pale.

All eyes were on Johnny now. "I never did

127

figure out what happened to the fence. I was ridin', then all of a sudden I seen 'em comin'. I shot off my gun an' yelled, but nobody heard me, an' it didn't have any effect on the cows.''

Lamson was hoarse. ''You mean . . . there was a drift? They got through the fence?''

''Yeah,'' Johnny said, ''but they are all right.''

''What do you mean''—Gavin's voice was icy—''all right? You mean I've got forty thousand dollars' worth of cattle piled up in the arroyo?''

''They ain't piled,'' Johnny explained. ''Not many, at least. I seen—saw—what was goin' to happen, so I got that powder out of the Rock House and blowed—I mean, I blew the edge of the arroyo. I figure they couldn't go no further, so they are probably scattered up an' down it.''

There was a long moment of deathly silence. Lamson was pale, the others incredulous. Gavin stared at Johnny, and after a minute he picked up his fork and started to eat. ''Let me get this straight,'' he said. ''You got ahead of the heard, blew off the edge of the arroyo, then got back and worked all night pointing those cattle toward the break?''

''It wasn't much.'' Johnny was sheepish. ''I had 'em narrowed down by the valley, so I just had to keep 'em that way.''

"I think that was wonderful!" the girl with the dark eyes said. "Don't you, Uncle Bart?"

"It saved me the best part of forty thousand dollars, is all." Gavin was emphatic. "Lamson, I want to talk to you. First, we'll take a look."

Of the more than a thousand cattle that drifted south, only six were lost. Despite the hurry and the darkness, Johnny had chosen his spot well and the powder had been well planted. Knowing the arroyo, he had known how many cracks were in the rocky edge, and how honeycombed it was with holes eroded by wind and water.

Gavin found his cattle scattered along the bottom of the arroyo, feeding on the rich grass that grew there where water often stood. He studied the blasted edge, glancing sharply at Johnny. "You knew something about powder, son," he said. "Those shots were well placed."

"My dad had a claim up in Oregon," Johnny explained. "I helped him some, doin' assignment work."

———

What Bart Gavin said to Lamson none of them knew, but for a few days his driving of Johnny ceased, although some sneering remarks about "pets" were made. And then gradually the old way resumed. It was Johnny Garrett who drew the rough jobs.

129

When there was to be a dance at Rock Springs Schoolhouse, where Johnny might have seen Mary Jane, he was sent to a line-camp at Eagle Rest.

It was a rugged, broken country, heavily timbered like his native Oregon, but riven by canyons and peaks, and cut here and there by lava flows and bordered on the east by the *malpais,* a forty-mile-wide stretch of lava where no horse could go and where a man's boots would be cut to ribbons in no time. Supposedly waterless, it was a treacherous area. There were stretches of flat, smooth lava, innocent in appearance, but actually that seemingly solid rock was merely the thin dome over a lava blister. Stepping on it, a man could plunge fifteen to fifty feet into a cavernous hole whose sides were slick and impossible to climb.

The few openings into this *malpais* were fenced, and the fences had to be kept up. At places the lava rode in a wall of basaltic blocks.

After the water holes were cleaned, salt scattered, and the fences checked, there was little to do. Johnny had a Colt and a Winchester, and he did a lot of shooting. He killed two mountain lions and a half-dozen wolves, skinning them and tanning the hides.

A week later Lasker rode in with two pack horses of supplies. Lasker was a tall, rawboned man who had punched cows for fifteen years.

He noticed the hides but made no comment. Hunkered down by the wall in the morning sun, he said, "Old man's worried. The tally fell off this year. He's losin' cows."

"You seen Mary Jane?"

"She was at the dance with Smoke," Lasker said, started to say something further, but stopped. Then he said, " 'Member that niece of Gavin's? She's livin' at the ranch. Her name is Betty."

"Too high-toned for any cowpunch."

"Can't tell about a woman," Lasker said. "Some of the high-toned ones are thoroughbreds."

———

Two days later Johnny found a dead cow. Wolves had torn it, but the cow had been shot in the head . . . the carcass not even a week old. Nobody had been around but Lasker and himself.

It was a Gavin cow. The only reason to shoot a cow was because she followed a rustled calf. Johnny was woods-bred and he spelled out the trail. A dozen head of young stuff had been taken through the timber into high country. He followed the scuffed trail through the pine needles, then lost it at the rim of a high canyon about the *malpais*.

For a week he scouted for sign, keeping up

the pretense of only doing his work. Once, he cut the trail of a shod horse but lost it. Back at the cabin he began to sketch a crude map on brown wrapping paper, incorporating all he knew of the country, marking ridges, arroyos, and streams.

Three small streams disappeared in the direction of the lava beds, and nobody had ever followed those streams to see where they went. Both streams were shallow—no water backed up anywhere.

The first stream, he discovered, veered suddenly south and dropped from sight in a deep cavern under the lava. Two days later, mending fence, he checked the next stream. It ended in a swamp.

Lasker and Lamson rode in the following day. Lasker was friendly and noticed the fresh wolf hide. "Good huntin'?"

"Yeah, but not enough time."

Smoke Lamson said nothing, but looked around carefully, and several times Johnny found Smoke watching him intently. It was not until they were about to leave that Lamson turned suddenly. "Seen anybody? Any strange riders?"

"Not a soul," Johnny told him, and after they were gone he swore at himself for not mentioning the tracks. And the cow.

———

On the third day after that, he circled around to trace the source of the one unexplored stream. When he found it he rode into the water and had followed it downstream more than a mile when he heard voices. He could distinguish no words, but two men were talking. Through a veil of brush he saw them ride out of the trees. One was a fat, sloppy man in a dirty gray shirt. The other was lean and savage; his name was Hoyt, and Johnny had seen him in town. He was said to be dangerous. After they were gone, Johnny followed cautiously.

The stream's current increased. It was dropping fast, and suddenly he found himself about to enter a sheer-walled canyon. Climbing his dun out of the water, he followed along the rim for more than an hour as the canyon grew deeper, until the riders were mere dots.

In a clearing atop the mountain, Johnny took his bearings. To north, south, and east lay the *malpais,* spotted with trees and brush that concealed the razorlike edges of broken lava. Suppose there was, far out there where the stream flowed, a grassy valley where stolen cattle were held?

Back at the cabin he made his decision. It was time to talk to Bart Gavin. Switching horses he rode back, arriving long after dark. It would take another day to return, but he must see the rancher. "Nobody home," the cook told him. "All gone to dance. Only Dan, he here."

Lasker sat up when Johnny walked into the bunkhouse. "Hey, what's up?" The sleep was gone from his eyes.

"Needed tobacco," Johnny lied glibly. He sat down. "A dance in town?"

Lasker relaxed. "So that's it? Kid, you'll get Lamson sore. You shouldn't oughta have come in."

"Aw, why not? Climb into your duds an' we'll ride. I want to see Mary Jane."

Riding into the outskirts, Lasker said, "That's a staked claim, kid. Better lay off." Then he added, "He's a fighter."

"So'm I. I grew up in lumber camps."

As they tied their horses, Lasker said again, "Stay away from Mary Jane. She ain't for you, kid, an'—"

Johnny turned to face him. "What's wrong with her?"

Lasker started to speak, then shrugged. "Your funeral."

Mary Jane squealed excitedly when she saw him. "Why, Johnny! I thought you were 'way up in the woods. What brought you back?"

"I had a reason." He liked being mysterious. "You'll know soon enough."

During the second dance she kept insisting.

"What reason, Johnny? Why did you come back?"

"Secret," he said. "You'll know before long."

"Tell me. I won't tell anybody."

"It's nothing." He shrugged it off. "Only I found some rustlers."

"You *found* them?" Her eyes were bright. "Why, John—!"

A big hand fell on his shoulder and he was spun into a hard fist crashing out of nowhere. He started to fall, but the second blow caught and knocked him sprawling.

Johnny's head was buzzing but he rolled over and got up swiftly. Smoke Lamson, his face hard and angry, swung wickedly, and Johnny clinched. Lamson hurled him to the floor, and before Johnny could scramble to his feet, Smoke rushed in and swung his leg for a kick. Johnny threw himself at Lamson's legs and they hit the floor in a heap. Coming up fast they walked into each other, punching with both hands. Johnny had the shorter reach but he got inside. He slammed a right to the ribs and Lamson took an involuntary step back. Then Johnny smashed a left to his face and, crouching, hooked a right to the body.

Around them the crowd was yelling and screaming. In the crowd was Mary Jane, her face excited, and nearby another face. That of the fat, sloppy man from the canyon!

Lamson rushed, but, over his momentary shock from the unexpected punch, Johnny was feeling good. Due to the brutally hard labor of the preceding fall and winter he was in fine shape. He was lithe as a panther and rugged as a Texas steer. He ducked suddenly and tackled Lamson. The big man fell hard and got up slowly. Johnny knocked him down. Lamson got up and Johnny threw him with a rolling hip-lock, and when the bigger man tried to get up again, Johnny knocked him down again.

His face bloody, Lamson stayed down. "Awright, kid. You whupped me."

Johnny backed off and then walked away. Mary Jane was nowhere in sight. Disappointed, he looked around again. Across the room he saw Gavin and his niece. Betty was looking at him, and she was smiling. He started toward them when something nudged his ribs and a cool voice said, "All right, kid, let's go outside an' talk."

"But I—"

"Right now. An' don't get any fancy ideas. You wouldn't be the first man I killed." The man with the gun in his back was Hoyt, the gun held so it could not be seen. They walked from the hall, and Betty looked after them, bewildered.

The fat rustler was waiting. He had Johnny's horse and theirs. Johnny moved toward his horse, remembering the pistol he had thrust into the saddlebag and the rifle in the scabbard. He reached for the pommel and a gun barrel came down over his skull. He started to fall, caught a second glancing blow, and dropped into a swirling darkness.

The lurching of the horse over the stones of the creek brought him to consciousness. The feel under his leg told him the rifle was gone. His ankles were tied, and his wrists. Was the pistol still in the saddlebag?

Pain racked his skull, and some time later he passed out again, coming out of it only when they took him off his horse and shoved him against the cabin wall. He was in a long grassy valley, ringed with *malpais,* but a valley of thousands of acres.

A third man came from the cabin. Johnny remembered him as cook for one of the roundup outfits, named Freck. "Grub's on," Freck said, nodding briefly at Johnny.

They ate in silence. Hoyt watched Johnny without making a point of it. Freck and the fat man ate noisily. "You tell anybody about this place?" Hoyt demanded.

"Maybe," Johnny said. "I might have."

"Horse comin'," Hoyt said suddenly. "See who it is, Calkins."

Johnny stiffened. Calkins . . . Mary Jane's father. Something died within him. He stared at his food, appetite gone. It had been Mary Jane, then, who told the rustlers he had found the cattle and the hideout. No wonder she had been curious. No wonder they had rushed him out before he could talk to Gavin.

Calkins stood in the door with a Winchester. Turning his head, he said, "It's the boss."

A hard, familiar voice called, then footsteps. Johnny saw Dan Lasker step into the door. Lasker's smile was bleak. "Hello, Johnny. It ain't good to see you."

"Never figured you for a rustler."

"Man can't get rich at forty a month, Johnny." He squatted on his heels against the wall. "We need another man." Lasker lit a smoke. He seemed worried. "You're here, kid."

It was a way out and there would be no other. And Lasker wanted him to take it. Actually speaking, there was no choice.

"Are you jokin'?" Johnny's voice was sarcastic. "Only thing I can't figure is why you didn't let me in on it from the start." And he lied quietly: "I was figurin' to moonlight a few cows myself, only I couldn't find a way out of the country."

Lasker was pleased. "Good boy, Johnny. As for a way out, we've got it."

138

Hoyt shoved back from the table. "All I can say is, one wrong move outa this kid, an' I'll handle it my own way!"

"All right, Hoyt." Lasker measured him coolly. "But be double-damned sure you're right."

They had over four hundred stolen cattle and were ready for a drive. But they did not return Johnny's guns. Nor did he make as much as a move toward his saddlebags.

———

Calkins came in midway of the following afternoon. He was puffing and excited. "Rider comin'. An' it's that young niece of Gavin's!"

Hoyt got up swiftly. "Dan, I don't like it!"

Freck walked to the door and waited there, watching her come. "What difference does it make? She's here, an' she ain't goin' back. Nobody ever found this place, and it's not likely they have now."

"What I want to know," Hoyt said bitterly, "is how she found it."

"Probably followed the kid." Lasker was uneasy and showed it. "She's sweet on him."

Betty Gavin was riding a black mare and she cantered up, smiling. "Hello, Johnny! Hello, Dan! Gee, I'm glad I found you! I thought I was lost."

"How'd you happen to get here?" Lasker inquired. He was puzzled. She seemed entirely unaware that anything was wrong. But being an eastern girl, how could she know? On the other hand, how could an eastern girl have got here?

"Uncle Bart was at the old place on Pocketpoint, so I decided I'd ride over and surprise Johnny. I lost my way, and then I saw some horse tracks, so I followed them. When I got in that canyon I was scared, but there was no way to get out, so I kept coming."

She looked around. "So this is what Eagle's Nest is like?"

Johnny Garrett was appalled. Calkins was frowning. Hoyt was frankly puzzled, as was Lasker. Yet Lasker looked relieved. He was not a murderer nor a man who would harm a woman, and this offered a way out. If Betty did not know the difference—

She came right up to Johnny, smiling. "My, but you're a mess!" she said. "Straighten your handkerchief." She reached up and pulled it around and he felt something sharp against the skin of his neck under the collar. It was a fold of paper. "Are you going to take me back to Pocketpoint?"

"Can't," he said. "But maybe Dan will. I'm busy here."

He scratched his neck, palmed the paper,

and when an opportunity offered, he got a glimpse of it. The paper was the brown wrapping paper upon which he had worked out his first map of the streams and the probable route into this valley, with his notes.

She had lied then. She had come from Eagle's Nest following his own map, and she knew exactly where she was! He looked at her in astonishment. How could she be so cool? So utterly innocent?

He began to roll a smoke, thinking this out. Lasker might take her out of here. He could be trusted with a woman, and the others could not. Out of the corners of his eyes, he measured the distance to the saddlebag. No good. They'd kill him before he got it open. Unless . . . He hesitated. Unless he was very careful about it—

———

Lasker, Calkins, and Hoyt had moved off to one side and were talking. Betty glanced at Johnny. "I was afraid I wouldn't find you," she said, low-voiced.

Freck could hear them, but there were two meanings here.

"Won't Bart be worried?"

"Yes, he probably will. I"—she looked right at him—"left a note at the cabin." *A note at the line cabin!* Then there was a chance!

Suddenly, Freck was speaking. "Hoyt," he said, "we better look at our hole card. That gal's got red mud on her boot. Ain't no place got red mud but around the cabin at Eagle's Nest."

Johnny felt his mouth go dry. He saw Betty's face change color, and he said quietly, "You don't know what you're sayin', Freck. There's red mud behind the cabin at Pocketpoint."

Hoyt looked at Calkins. "Is there? You been there?"

"I been there. Dogged if I can recall!"

Hoyt's eyes were suddenly hard. He turned a little so his lank body was toward Lasker. Almost instinctively, Calkins drew back, but Freck's loyalty to Hoyt was obvious.

"Got a present for you, Betty." Johnny spoke into the sudden silence. His voice seemed unusually loud. "Aimed to bring it down first chance I got. One of those agates I was tellin' you about."

He walked to his saddlebag, and behind him he heard Hoyt say, "We can't let that girl leave here, Dan."

"Don't be a fool!" Lasker's anger was plain. "You can steal cattle and get away with it. Harm a girl like this and the West isn't big enough to hide us!"

"I'll gamble. But if she goes out, we're finished. Our work done for nothin'."

"Keep her," Freck said. "She'd be company." He winked at Lasker.

All eyes were watching Hoyt. It was there the trouble would start. Johnny ran his hand down into the saddlebag and came up with the .44 Colt. He turned, the gun concealed by his body.

"She goes," Lasker said, "cattle or no cattle."

"Over my dead body!" Hoyt snapped, and his hand dropped for his gun.

Freck grabbed iron, too, and Johnny yelled. The cook swung his head and Johnny's pistol came up. Johnny shot and swung his gun. Calkins backed away, hands high and his head shaking.

Guns were barking, and Johnny turned. Lasker was down and Hoyt was weaving on his feet. Hoyt stared at Lasker. "We had him, Freck an' me, just like we figured! Had him boxed, in a cross-fire! Then you—!" His gun came up and Johnny fired, then fired again. Hoyt went down and rolled over.

Johnny wheeled on Calkins. "Drop your belt!" His voice was hard. "Now get in there an' get some hot water!"

He moved swiftly to Betty. "Are you all right?"

Her face was pale, her eyes wide and

shocked. "All right," she whispered. "I'll be all right."

Johnny ran to Lasker. The cowhand lay sprawled on the ground and he had been shot twice. Once through the chest, once through the side. But he was still alive. . . .

———

Bart Gavin and four hands rode in an hour later. Gavin stopped abruptly when he saw the bodies, then came on in. Betty ran to him.

Johnny came to the door. "Me an' Dan," he said, "we had us a run-in with some rustlers. In the shootout Dan was wounded. With luck, he'll make it."

Bart Gavin had one arm around his niece. "Betty saw Hoyt take you out, but we thought she was imagining things, so when she couldn't make us believe, she took off on her own. Naturally, we trailed her . . . and found her note and your map, traced out."

Gavin saw Calkins. His face grew stern. "What's he doin' here?"

Johnny said quietly, "He stayed out of it. He was rustlin', but when it came to Betty, he stayed out. I told him we'd let him go."

Inside the cabin they stood over Lasker. He was conscious, and he looked up at them. "That was white, mighty white of you."

144

"Need you," Johnny said quietly. "Gavin just told me he fired Lamson. He said he'd been watchin' my work, an' I'm the new foreman. You're workin' for me now."

"For us," Betty said. "As long as he wants."

Lasker grinned faintly. "Remember what I said, kid? That some of the high-toned gals were thoroughbreds?"

No Rest
for the Wicked

Author's Note

It takes two kinds of men to develop a mining country: the men who find the mines and the men who develop them, and they are rarely the same person. The prospector, the discoverer, is not often equipped in money and the business ability to open up and develop a mine. Many of them sold their claim off for what seemed nothing. And yet it was to them a great deal. And if they'd persisted in operating their mines they might have lost everything.

Some men only wanted what they could take out by themselves. They kept their discoveries a secret, going back again and again to take out what they needed, and when they died—of disease, accident, or gun play—the mine's location was lost.

From the ridge on my Colorado ranch I can look across a bunch of mountains where there are dozens of lost mines. At least two of them are somewhere in the range of my vision. Find them? It isn't easy. It's a big, big country and prospecting is a slow, painstaking operation. Since prospectors gave up the burro for the Jeep, fewer mines are found. Jeeps can't go into the roughest country, and many of the best mines were found at places where no man in his right mind would want to go.

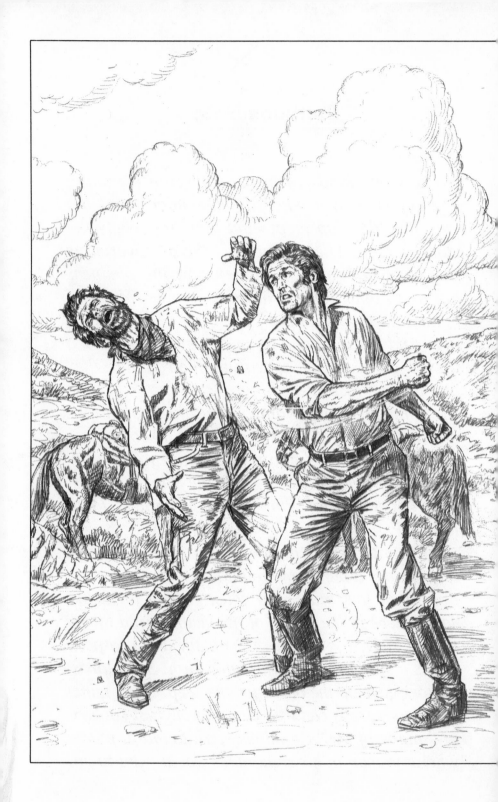

The bat-wing doors slammed open as if struck by a charging steer and he stood there, framed for an instant in the doorway, a huge man with a golden beard and magnificent shoulders.

Towering five inches over six feet and weighing no less than two hundred and fifty pounds, he appeared from out of the desert like some suddenly reincarnated primeval giant.

He was dirty, not with the dirt of indigence, but with the dust and grime of travel. He smelled of the trail, and his cheekbones had a desert bronze upon them. As he strode to the bar there was something reckless and arrogant about him that raised the hackles on the back of my neck.

Stopping near me he called for a bottle, and when he had it in his hand he poured three fingers into a water glass and took it neat. He followed with its twin before he paused to look around.

He glanced at the tables where men played cards, and then at the roulette wheel. His eyes rested on the faces of the gamblers, and then at last, they swung around to me. Oh, I knew he was coming to me! He had seen me when he came in, but he saved me for last.

His look measured me and assayed me with a long, deliberately contemptuous glance. For I am a big man, too, and the difference between us was slight.

Yet where he was golden, I was black, and where the heat had reddened his cheekbones, I was deep-browned by sun and wind. We measured each other like two stranger mastiffs, and neither of us liked the other.

He looked from my eyes to the star on my chest, and to the gun low-slung on my leg. He grinned then, a slow, insulting grin. "The town clown," he said.

"Exactly," I replied, and smiled at him. For I could see it then, knew it was coming, and I could afford to wait. He measured me again when he saw that I did not anger.

He changed suddenly, shrugging, and smiled. "No offense," he said, and his smile seemed genuine. "I've got a loose tongue." He reached in his pocket and drew out three pieces of ore and rolled them on the bar. "Besides, I feel too good to make trouble for anybody today. I've found the Lost Village Diggings."

His voice had not lifted a note, and yet had he shouted the words he could have received no more attention. Every head turned; men came to their feet; all eyes were on him, all ears listening.

"The Lost Village Diggings!" Old Tom Curtis grabbed the stranger by the arm. "You've found 'em? You actually have? Where?"

The big man chuckled. "Didn't aim to get you folks upset," he said. "Look for yourself." He nudged the ore with his fist. "How's that look?"

Curtis grabbed up the ore. His eyes were hot with excitement. He was almost moaning in his reverence. "Why! Why, it must run three or four thousand dollars to the ton! *Look* at it!"

The chunks of ore were ribbed with gold, bright and lovely to see, but I spared the gold only a glance. My eyes were on the stranger, and I was waiting.

They crowded around him, shouting their questions, eager to see and to handle the ore. He poured another drink, looked at me, then grinned. He lifted the glass in a silent toast.

Yet I think it bothered him. The rest of them were crazy with gold fever, but I was not. And he didn't understand it.

The Lost Village Diggings! Stories of lost mines crop up wherever one goes in the South-west, but this one was even more fantastic than most. In 1609 three Franciscan friars, accompanied by an officer and sixteen soldiers, started north out of Mexico.

Attacked by Apaches, they turned back, and finally were surrounded among rough mountains by the Indians. During the night they attempted to escape and became lost. By daylight they found themselves moving through utterly strange country, and their directions seemed all wrong. All of them felt curiously confused.

Yet they had escaped the Indians. Thankfully, they kept on, getting deeper and deeper into unfamiliar country. On the third day they found themselves in a long canyon through which wound a stream of fresh, clear water. There were wide green meadows, rich soil, and a scattering of trees. Weary of their flight, they gratefully settled down for a rest. And then they found gold.

The result was, instead of going on, they built houses and a church, and remained to mine the rich ore, and reduce it to raw gold. Accompanied by one of the Indians who had come with them, for there had been a dozen of these, four soldiers attempted to find a way out to Mexico. All were killed but one, who returned. Attracted by the healing of one of the Franciscans, several Tarahumares came to live

154

among them, and then more. Several of the soldiers took wives from the Indian girls and settled down. Lost to the outside world, the village grew, cultivated fields, and was fairly prosperous. And they continued to mine gold.

Yet a second attempt to get out of the valley also failed, with three men killed. It was only after thirty years had passed that an Indian succeeded. He got through to Mexico and reported the village. Guiding the party on the return trip, he was bitten by a snake and died.

In 1750 two wandering Spanish travelers stumbled upon a faint trail and followed it to the village. It had grown to a tight, neatly arranged settlement of more than one hundred inhabitants. The travelers left, taking several villagers with them, but they likewise were killed by Apaches. Only one man got through, adding his story to the legend of the Lost Village. From that day on it was never heard of again.

"All my life," Old Tom Curtis said, "I've hoped I'd find that Village! Millions! Millions in gold there, all stored and waiting to be took! A rich mine! Maybe several of 'em!"

The big man with the golden beard straightened up. "My name's Larik Feist," he said. "I found the Lost Village by accident. I was back in the Sierra Madres, and I wounded a boar. I chased after him, got lost, and just stumbled on her."

"Folks still there?" Curtis asked eagerly.

"Nobody," Feist said. "Not a soul. Dead for years, looks like." He leaned against the bar and added three fingers to his glass. "But I found the mine—two of 'em! I found their *arrastra*, too!"

"But the gold?" That was Bob Wright, owner of the livery stable. "Did you find the gold?"

"Not yet," Feist admitted, "but she's got to be there."

There was an excited buzz of talk, but I turned away and leaned against the bar. There was nothing I could say, and nobody who would believe me. I knew men with the gold fever; I'd seen others have it. So I waited, knowing what was coming, and thinking about Larik Feist.

"Sure," Feist said, "I'm goin' back. Think I'm crazy? Apaches? Never seen a one, but what if I did? No Apache will keep me away from there. But I got to get an outfit."

"I'll stake you," Wright said quickly. "I'll furnish the horses and mules."

Men crowded around, tendering supplies, equipment, guns, experience. Feist didn't accept; he just shook his head. "First thing I need," he said, "is some rest. I won't even think about it until morning."

He straightened up and gathered his samples. Reluctantly, the others drew back. Feist looked over at me. "What's the matter, Marshal?" he taunted. "No gold fever?"

"Once," I said, "I had it."

"He sure did!" Old Tom Curtis chuckled. "Why, he was only a boy, but he sure spent some time down there. Say! He'd be a good man to take along! The marshal sure knows the Sierra Madres!"

Feist had started to move away. Now he stopped. His face had a queer look. "You've been there?" he demanded.

"Yes." I spoke quietly. "I've been there."

———

That was the beginning of it. Larik Feist avoided me, but his plans went forward rapidly. A company was formed with Feist as president, Wright as treasurer, and Dave Neil as vice-president. When I heard that, I walked down to Neil's house. Marla was out in the yard, picking flowers.

"Your dad home?"

She straightened and nodded to me. It seemed she was absent-minded—not like she usually was when I came around. I stood there, and I looked myself over in her eyes. I was a big man, two inches shorter than Feist, and maybe twenty pounds less in weight. Yet I'm mighty spare and muscular, and folks generally figure me to weigh no more than two hundred and a few pounds.

So I knew what she saw, a big man with wide, thick shoulders and a chest that stretched his shirt tight. With a brown, wind-darkened face and green eyes, a shock of black, curly, and unusually untrimmed hair, a battered black sombrero, flat crowned, a faded checked shirt, jeans, and boots with run-down heels. And two big guns that looked small on me.

Feist was different. He had the trail dust off him now and a new outfit of clothes, bought on credit. He looked slick and handsome; his hair was trimmed. He was the talk of the town, with all the girls making big eyes at him. They all knew me. They all knew Lou Morgan, who was half-Irish and half-Spanish.

"Yes, Dad's inside talking to Larik," she said. "Isn't he wonderful?"

That hurt. Marla? Well, I'd always figured on Marla being my girl. We'd gone dancing together, we'd been riding together, and we'd talked some about the future—when I'd made my stake and owned a ranch.

"Wonderful?" I shook my head. "That doesn't seem like the right word."

"Oh, Lou!" She was impatient. "Don't be like that! Here Larik comes to town and offers us all a chance to be rich, and you stand around—they all told me how you acted—just like . . . like . . . like you were jealous of him!''

''Why should I be jealous?'' I asked.

Her eyes chilled a little. ''Oh? You don't think I'm worth being jealous over?''

That made me look at her again. ''Oh! So you're in this, too? It's not only all the town's money he wants, but you, too.''

''You've no right to talk that way! I like Larik! He's wonderful! And he's doing something for us all!''

Right then I couldn't trust myself to talk. I just walked by her and went into the house. Neil was there, seated at the table with Feist, Wright, Curtis, and John Powers. They all had money on the table, and some sort of legal-looking papers.

''What's the money for?'' I asked, quiet-like.

''We're buyin' into Mr. Feist's mine,'' Powers said. ''You'd better dig down in that sock of yours and get a piece of this, Lou. We'll need a good man to protect that gold.'' Powers turned to Feist and jerked a head at me. ''Lou, here, is about the fastest thing with a gun this side of Dodge.''

Feist looked up at me, his eyes suddenly cold and careful.

159

Me, I didn't look at him. "Neil," I said, "do you mean to tell me you men are all paying good cash for something you've never seen? That you're buyin' a pig in a poke?"

"Never seen?" Neil said. "What does that matter? We've seen the gold, haven't we? We all know the Lost Village story, and—"

"All you know," I said, "is an old legend that's been told around for years. You're all like a pack of kids taken in by a slick-talking stranger. Feist"—I looked across the table at him—"you're under arrest. Obtaining money under false pretenses."

Neil lunged to his feet. His face was flushed with anger. "Lou, what's the matter? Have you gone crazy?"

All of them were on their feet protesting. Only Larik Feist had not moved, but for the first time he looked worried.

It was Marla who made it worse. "Dad," she said, "pay no attention to him. Lou's jealous. He's made big tracks around here so long he can't stand for anybody to take the limelight."

That made me red around the gills because it was so untrue. "You think what you like, but I'm taking Feist now."

Feist looked at me, a long measuring look from those cold, careful eyes. He had it in his mind.

"Don't go for that gun," I said quietly. "I want you tried in a court of law, not dead on this floor."

Powers put a hand on Feist's arm. "Go along with him," he said. "And don't worry. We'll take care of you. Far as that goes, we can call a meeting and throw him out of office."

"I'm arresting Feist," I said patiently. "You do whatever you want."

"On what evidence?" Neil demanded.

"I'll present the evidence when it's needed," I said. "Take my word for it, I've evidence for a conviction. This man has never been to Lost Village. He didn't get his gold there. And there's no gold there, anyway, but a little placer stuff."

Whether they heard me or not, I don't know. They were all around me, yelling at me, shaking their fingers in my face. And they were all mad. Neil was probably the maddest of all. Marla, when I looked at her, just turned her head away.

Feist got up when I told him to, and walked out ahead of me. "I might have expected this," he said. "But you won't get away with it."

"Yes, I will. And when they discover what you tried to put over, I'll have trouble keeping you from getting lynched."

When he was locked in a cell, I walked back to my desk and sat down.

Ever feel like the whole world was against you? Well, that's the way I felt then. My girl had turned her back on me. The town's leading citizens—the men I'd worked for, been friends with and protected—they all hated me. And they could throw me out of office, that was true. All they needed was to get the council together.

It was ten miles to the nearest telegraph, but when the stage went out that night, I had a letter on it.

Up and down the street men were gathered in knots, and when they looked at me they glared and muttered. So I walked back to my office and sat down. Feist was stretched on his cot, and he never moved.

Every night now, for months, Marla Neil had brought me a pot of coffee at eight o'clock. When eight drew near, I began to feel both hungry and miserable. There'd be no Marla tonight, that was something I could bet. And then, there she was, a little cool, but with her coffeepot.

"Marla!" I sat up straight. "Then you—?" I got to my feet. "You're not mad at me? Believe me, Marla, when you all know the truth, you won't be. Listen, I can ex—"

She drew back. "Drink your coffee," she said, "or it will get cold. I'll talk to you tomorrow." She turned and hurried away.

162

So I sat down, ate a cookie, and then poured out the coffee. It was black and strong, the way I like it . . . very black, and very strong. . . .

———

My mouth tasted funny, when I awoke, and I had trouble getting my eyes open. When I got them open I rolled and caught myself just in time. It wasn't my bed I was in. I was on a jail cot.

My head felt like it weighed a ton, but I lifted it and looked around. I was in a cell. Larik Feist's cell.

That brought me to my feet with a lurch. I charged the door.

Locked.

Taking that door in my two hands I shook it until the whole door rattled and banged. I shouted, but there was no sound from outside. I swore. Then I looked around. There was a note on the floor.

I picked it up and read:

You wouldn't listen to us. I hated to do this, but you'd no right to keep the whole town from getting rich just because of your pigheaded jealousy.

It didn't need any signature, for by that time

I was remembering that the last thing I had done was drink some coffee Marla had brought me.

The door rattled and I yelled, but nobody answered. I went to the window and looked out. Nobody was stirring, but I knew all those who lived in town weren't gone. They probably had orders to ignore me.

Then I remembered something else. This jail was old and of adobe. I'd been trying for months to get the council to vote the money to make repairs. These bars— As I've said, I weigh two hundred and thirty pounds and none of it anything but bone and muscle. I grabbed those bars and bowed my back, but they wouldn't stir. Yet I knew they weren't well seated. Then I picked up the cot and smashed it, and taking one of the short iron pieces, I used it as a lever between the bars. That did the trick.

In five minutes I was on the street, then back inside after my guns. This time I belted on two of them, grabbed my Winchester, and ran for the livery stable.

Abel was there, but no Wright. I grabbed Abel. "Which way did they go?" I yelled at him.

"Lou!" he protested, pulling back. "You let go of me. I ain't done nothing! And you leave those folks alone. We all going to be rich."

I dropped him, because I remembered something very suddenly. Larik Feist had changed his clothes after he came to town. Had he taken the old ones with him after he got a complete outfit? I made a run for Powers' store, but it was closed. I put one foot against the door jamb and took the knob in my hands— It came loose, splintering the jamb.

The clothes were there. A worn, dirty shirt, jeans, boots, and a coat. Right there I sat down and looked them over.

Not that I didn't know where they were going now. The Sierra Madres were far south of the border, and nobody except a few Indians and Mexicans who live there knew them better than I. What I wanted to know was where Feist had come from, because one thing I knew. He had not come up from Mexico.

From our town the country slopes gradually away to the Border. It's a long valley running deep into Mexico, and from my usual seat at the jail door I could look down that valley. Yesterday, before Feist appeared, I had been sitting there, and Larik Feist had not come up that valley. Nothing bigger than a mouse or rattlesnake had been moving out there.

Now, just before noon, Luke Fair drove his buckboard in from Tombstone, and he had seen nobody for fifty miles, he said. The fact remained, all things considered, the only way Feist could have come was by train. The railroad was just ten miles away. And I'd spotted soot on his ears, which he'd not washed off.

The dust on his clothes was not desert dust—no more than he could have picked up coming from the railroad. And there were some cinders in the cuffs of his jeans. All his clothes were old except for the coat. It had a label from an El Paso store.

Tracking that party into Mexico offered no problem, but I had another idea. Feist, if I was right, and I was betting my shirt on it, would get his hands on the money that had been put up. Then he would light out and leave them stranded. And I had just a hunch where he would go.

Luke Fair was in front of his shack when I walked up. "You played hob," he said.

I spoke fast: "Luke, get a horse and a couple of pack mules. Take grub and plenty of water. Then light out after that bunch. By the time you get to them, they'll be mighty glad to see you."

Luke looked at me. The fact that he was here and not with them showed he had brains. "What do you mean?"

"I mean," I said, "that about fifty miles south of the Border you'll find that bunch. They'll probably be out of water and afoot."

He took his pipe out of his mouth. "I don't get you."

"That Feist," I said, "was a swindler. He never saw the Sierra Madres. I'd bet a coon he never. He rigged that story, and that gold never came from Lost Village because there's no gold there, and never was."

"How do you know that?"

"Luke, what was my ma's name?"

"Why"—he looked sort of odd—"it was Ibañez."

"Sure, and Luke, do you know what the name of that officer was who went with the Franciscan friars?"

"No."

"It was Ibañez. Luke, I've had a map to Lost Village ever since I was six. My father went there when he was a boy. I went there, too. There was a village, but folks left it when the springs went dry. There never was any mining close by. The mine they took the gold from was ten miles from the village itself, and it's being worked right now by the Sonora Mining Company."

"Well, I'll be blasted!" Luke just sat there looking at me. "Why didn't you tell them?"

"I started to, but they wouldn't listen. Most of it I didn't want to tell until the trial. I didn't want this gent to know what he was facing. I had no idea they'd go off the way they did."

"If I was you," he said, "I'd let 'em get back the best they can."

"They might not get back," I told him, but he knew that as well as I did. He got up and began gathering his duffel.

"What about you?" he asked.

That made me grin. "Luke, that gent will head for El Paso unless I'm clean off my rocker. He'll ditch them about the second day out and he'll head through the hills toward El Paso. He'll take a straight route, and about noon of the second day after he leaves them, he'll stop for water at a little *pozo*, a place called Coyote Spring. And, Luke, when he gets there, I'll be sitting close by."

———

If you look on a good big map, and if you pick a place about midway between the Animas and the Alamo Huaco Mountains, and then measure off about twenty-eight miles or so south of the border, you'll find Pozo de Coyote.

The spring is in a plain, but the country is rough and broken, and the ground slopes off a little into a sort of hollow. The *pozo* is in the bottom. At noon, on the second day after I figured Larik Feist would have left them, I was sitting back in the brush with my field glasses and a rifle.

He was more than an hour late getting to the *pozo,* but I was taking it easy back in a tall clump of cholla and mesquite when I heard his horse. It was hot—a still, blazing noon in the desert when he drew up at the water hole. Lifting my Winchester, I put a bullet into the sand at his feet. He jerked around and jumped for his rifle, but as he lifted it, I smashed two shots at the stock and he dropped it as if it was hot. The stock was splintered. He stood stock-still, his hands lifted.

Getting to my feet, I walked down the hill. Once he made a motion as if to go for his gun, but I fired the rifle from the hip and grooved the leather of his holster. When I stepped into the open we were thirty yards apart.

His face was flushed with heat and fury, and he glared at me, the hatred a living thing in his eyes. "You, is it? I might have guessed."

"What kept you so long, Feist?" I said. "I've been waiting for you."

"How'd you get here? How'd you know I'd be coming this way?"

"Simple." I smiled at him, taking my time. Then I let him have it, about the map I had, how the Lost Village was not lost, and how there was no mine at all there, and no gold, and never had been.

"So you knew all the time?" It made him

169

furious to think that. "Now what are you going to do?"

"Take you in. I wired Tucson about you. They are checking with other places. You'll be wanted some place." My rifle tilted a little. "Drop your gun belts," I told him. "Or, if you feel lucky, try to draw."

Gingerly, he moved his hands to his belt buckle, and unfastening it, he let the belt drop. Then, stepping carefully, he moved away. I closed in and picked up the belt, then shucked shells from the gun, and stuck the belt and gun in my saddlebag. Then I spoke again to Larik Feist: "Now get ready to travel, fellow."

———

Three days later I rode into town with Larik Feist tied to his saddle. He had made one break to escape, and had taken a bad beating. His eyes were swollen shut and his beard matted with blood and sand. He looked like he had been dragged through a lava bed on his face.

There was nobody in sight. Soon a few people, mostly women, came to the doors to watch.

Luke Fair strolled out finally. I handed him the pouch containing the money I'd recovered.

"Where's everybody? Did you find 'em?"

Fair grinned at me. "Found 'em just like

170

you said, afoot and out of water. He'd stolen their horses and canteens, but I rounded up the horses that he'd turned loose, and we started back.''

''But where are they?''

He chuckled. ''Mining,'' he said. ''Working one of the richest ledges I ever saw. We started back, but about ten miles below the border, Powers sits down for a rest and crumbles a piece of rotten quartz, and it was fairly alive with gold. So they all staked claims an' they all figure that they're going to get rich.''

He started to walk toward the bank, then stopped. ''Marla's in town,'' he said.

When I'd jailed Feist, I thought about it. Suddenly, I knew what I was doing. The law could have Feist and they could have their marshal's job.

———

Marla opened the door for me, and she'd never looked prettier. Some of it was last-minute fixin'—I could easily see that.

My badge was in my hand. ''Give that to your dad,'' I said. ''He and Powers wanted a new marshal—now they can get him.''

''But they were angry, Lou!'' she protested. ''They weren't thinking!''

''Be the same way next time. Feist is in

jail. You can turn him over to the law, or hang him, or let him rot there, or turn him loose, for all of me.''

Marla looked at me. She didn't know what to say. She was pretty and she knew it, but suddenly that meant nothing at all to me and she saw it. And believe me, it was the only thing she had, the only weapon and the only asset. I could see that then, which I couldn't see before.

"Where are you going?'' she asked, hesitantly.

My horse was standing there and I stepped into the saddle. "Why," I said, "I've been setting here since I was a kid talking to folks who'd been places. Once I made a trip to Tombstone, but this time, I'm really traveling. I'm going clear to Tucson!"

So I rode out of town, and I never looked back.

Not once.

That
Packsaddle Affair

■————————————————■————————————————■

Author's Note

One of the things you didn't do in the West was bother a woman. It rarely happened.

Women were scarce and valued accordingly. A lot of men grew up reading the novels of Sir Walter Scott and they adopted the author's notions of chivalry. There are many, many accounts in diaries and elsewhere of women traveling back and forth across the West alone and never being disturbed in the least.

If a woman got off a stage at a stage-stop to get something to eat, and a man didn't get up to give her a place at the table, somebody else knocked him off the seat so she could be seated. You couldn't even bump into a woman walking in the street without somebody knocking you into the ground for it.

Women were treated with great respect and this was universal all over the frontier. It was one thing you didn't transgress.

Red Clanahan, a massive man with huge shoulders and a wide-jawed face, was no longer in a hurry. The energetic posse which had clung so persistently to his trail had been left behind on the Pecos. Their horses had played out and two of them were carrying double.

Red had pushed on to Lincoln, where he'd swapped his sorrel for a long-legged, deep-chested black with three white stockings. Then with only time out for a quick meal and a changing of saddles, he'd headed west for the Rio Grande and beyond it, the forks of the Gila.

Packsaddle Stage Station was a long, low building of adobe, an equally long, low stable, and two pole corrals. There was a stack of last year's hay and a fenced-in pasture where several stage horses grazed, placid in the warm morning sun. Three saddled horses stood three-legged at the hitch-rail, and a drowsy Mexican, already warming up for his siesta, sat in the shade alongside the building.

Slipping the thongs from his pistol butt, Clanahan rode down the last hundred yards to the station and dismounted at the trough. Keeping his horse between himself and the station, he loosened the cinch a little and then led the horse to a patch of grass in the shade alongside the trail. Only then did he start for the station.

A narrow-shouldered man with a thin wolf's face had come from the stage station and was watching him. He wore a gun butt forward in a right-side holster, which might be used for either the left or right hand.

"Come down the trail?" he asked, his narrow eyes taking in Clanahan with cool attention.

"Part way. Came down from the Forks and across the Flat."

"Stage is late." The tall man still watched him. "Wondered if you'd seen it?"

"No." Clanahan walked on by and opened the station door. It was cool and shadowed inside. There were several tables, chairs, and a twenty-foot bar at which two men lounged, talking to the barkeep. Another man sat at a table in the farthest corner. Both the men at the bar looked rough and trail-wise.

Red Clanahan moved to the end of the bar

and stopped there where he could watch all the men and the door as well. "Rye," he said, when the bartender glanced his way.

As he waited, he rested his big hands on the bar and managed a glance toward the silent man in the corner. The man just sat there with his hands clasped loosely on the table, unmoving. He wore a hat that left only his mouth and chin visible at this distance and in this light. He wore a string tie and a frock coat.

There was a situation here that Red could not fathom, but he realized he had walked into something happening or about to happen— probably connected with the arrival of the stage.

The man from outside came back in. His hips were wider than his shoulders and the holster gave him a peculiarly lopsided appearance.

Red Clanahan had a shock of red hair and a red-brown face with cold green eyes above high, flat cheekbones. Once seen, he was not easily forgotten, for he was six feet three and weighed an easy two hundred and thirty pounds. And there were places where he was not only known, but wanted.

There was a matter of some cattle over in Texas. Red's father had died while he was away, and when he returned he found that the three thousand head his father had tallied, shortly before his death, had mysteriously been ab-

sorbed by two larger herds. With no legal chan-
nels of recovery open to him, Red had chosen
illegal methods, and one thing had led to another. Red Clanahan was high on the list of
men wanted in Texas.

He finished his drink and had another. Then
he looked over at the bartender. "How about
some grub?"

The bartender was a big man, too, with a
round face and two chins but small, twinkling
eyes and a bald head. He removed his cigar and
nodded. "When the stage comes in—'most any
time."

The two men turned to look at him. Then the
tall man looked around at the bartender. "Feed
him now, Tom. Maybe he wants to ride on."

Red glanced up, his cold green eyes on the
speaker. "I can wait," he said coolly.

One of the other men turned. He was short
and thickset, with a scar on his jaw. "Maybe
we don't want you to wait," he said.

Red Clanahan looked into the smaller man's
eyes for a long, slow minute. "I don't give a
royal damn what you want," he said quietly.
"Whatever you boys are cookin', don't get it in
my way or I'll bust up your playhouse."

He reached for the bottle and drew it nearer
as the short man started toward him. "Listen,
you—"

He came one step too close and Red Clanahan hit him across the mouth with the back of his big hand. The blow seemed no more than a gesture but it knocked the shorter man sprawling across the room, his lips a bloody pulp.

Red met the gaze of the other men without moving or turning a hair. "Want in?" he said. "I'm not huntin' trouble but maybe you're askin' for it."

The tall man with the narrow shoulders looked ugly. "You swing a wide loop, stranger. Perhaps you're cuttin' into something too big for you."

"I doubt it."

His cool assurance worried Ebb Fallon. They had a job to do, and starting a fight with this stranger was no way to do it. Who was the man? Fallon stared at him, trying to remember. He was somebody, no doubt about that.

Shorty Taber got up slowly from the floor. Still dazed, he touched his fingers to his crushed lips and stared at the blood. Pure hatred was in his eyes as he looked up at Clanahan.

"I'll kill you for that," Taber said.

Red Clanahan reached for the bottle and filled his glass. "Better stick to punchin' cows," he said. "Quit goin' around pickin' fights with strangers. You'll live longer."

Taber glared at him and his right hand

dropped a fraction. Red was looking at him, still holding the bottle. "Don't try it," he warned. "I could take a drink and shoot both your ears off before you cleared leather."

Taber hesitated, then turned and walked to his friends. They whispered among themselves for a few minutes while the bartender polished a glass. Through it all, the man at the table had not moved. In the brief silence there was a distant pounding of hoofs and a rattle of wheels.

Instantly, two of the three turned to the door. The third stepped back and dropped into a chair near the wall, but facing the door. The bartender looked nervously at Red Clanahan. "We'll serve grub when the passengers arrive," he said. "They change teams here."

The stage drew up out front and then the door opened. Two men and a woman came in, and then a girl. She was slender and tall, with large violet eyes. She looked quickly toward the bar. Then her eyes touched fleetingly on Red's face, and she went on to the table and seated herself there. Obviously, she was disturbed.

Red Clanahan saw her eyes go to the third of the three riders, the fattish man who had remained indoors. Red happened to turn his head slightly and was shocked by the expression on the bartender's face. He was dead-white and his brow was beaded with sweat.

The passengers ate quietly. Finally the driver came in, had a drink, and turned. "Rolling!" he called. "Let's go!"

All got to their feet, and as they did, Ebb Fallon walked to the door, standing where the passengers had to brush him to get by. The girl was last to leave. As she turned to the door, the man at the nearby table got up.

"All right, Ebb," he said, "tell 'em to roll it."

He moved toward the girl. "My name's Porter, ma'am. You'd best sit down."

"But I've got to get on the stage!" she protested indignantly. "I can't stay."

She started past him and Porter caught her wrist. "Came to see your father, didn't you?" the man said. "Well, he's here."

That stopped her. Outside the stage was in motion; then they heard it go down the trail. When the rumble of wheels had died away, the door of the station opened, and Taber stepped in. He looked at the bartender, then at Red. His eyes shifted on to the girl.

"Well, where is he?" she demanded.

Ebb Fallon lifted his hand and pointed to the man seated at the table in the corner. But before the girl could move, the bartender put one hand on the bar. "Ma'am," he said, his voice strangely gentle, "don't go to that man.

183

They are tryin' to trick you. They want the claim.''

"But, I—" She looked from one to the other. "I don't understand."

Fallon had turned on the bartender, and as he looked across the hardwood at him, his eyes were devilish. "I'll kill you for that, Sam."

"Not while I'm here," Red Clanahan said.

Fallon's face turned dark. "You keep out of this!" he flared. "Be glad you got off so easy before!"

Red continued to lean on the bar. "Ma'am," he said, "I've no idea what this is all about, but I'm your friend."

The girl turned sharply and went to the man in the corner. Yet as her hand touched him, he fell slowly forward, his hat rolling to the floor. He slumped on the table, his cheek against the table top. His eyes were wide and staring. Over one eye was a blue hole.

She stared back in horror. "Dan! That's Dan Moore, Daddy's friend!"

"That *was* Dan Moore," Fallon replied. "You come with us, ma'am."

Fallon started toward her and she shrank back. Shorty Taber and Porter turned suddenly on the bartender and Red. "Just stay where you are, you two. This girl goes with us. She'll be all right," he added. "We just want some information and then she can go on her way.''

Red Clanahan straightened at the bar and reached for the bottle. Coolly, he poured a drink. ''You're wastin' your time,'' he said patiently. ''She doesn't know anything about it and never did.''

Ebb Fallon turned sharply. ''What's that? What did you say?''

''You heard me right. She knows nothing about the claim. Whoever hired you sure picked the dumbest help he could find. First you kill the one man who could help you; then you risk hell by kidnapin' this girl off that stage. And she not knowin' a thing!''

He looked from Fallon to Porter, his eyes cold with contempt. ''Ever stop to think what'll happen when that stage reaches the end of the line and that driver finds she was taken off here? If you recall, western folks don't take to men troublin' women.'' He filled his glass. ''I look to see you hang.''

''Who are you?'' Fallon persisted. ''What do you know about this?''

''Who I am doesn't matter,'' Red replied, ''except that I'm tougher than the three of you and would admire to prove it. But I'll tell you this: you did a blundering job of killing this girl's father. He wasn't dead when you left him.''

"*What?*" Fallon's face was livid. "What's that?"

"I said he wasn't dead. He got into a saddle and rode all of ten miles before he passed out. He was a game man. I found him on the trail, cared for him—sat with him until he died. That was about daybreak this mornin'."

"I don't believe it!" Taber burst out. "You're lyin'!"

Clanahan glanced at Taber. "Do you want to get slapped around some more? I'd enjoy doin' it."

Taber stepped back, his gun barrel lifting. "You try it!" he snarled. "I'll kill you!"

Red ignored him. "Her pa told me about the claim. Told me where it was, all about it." He smiled. "Fact is, I was there this mornin', and if you want to talk business, get your boss down here with some cash."

"Cash?"

"I'm sellin' my information," Red replied, "for fifteen thousand dollars."

"But that claim belongs to the girl!" the bartender protested.

"Not if they get down there first and change the stakes and filin' notice." Red Clanahan shrugged, and gave Sam a half smile. "You get your boss down here with some money."

They hesitated, not liking it. Yet Red could see that they were worried. The blunders they had made were now obvious to them, and there was a good chance the girl did not know where the claim was. "Don't trust him," Taber said. "There's something fishy about this."

Clanahan chuckled. "You boys figure it out, but be fast. I don't have much time. If it wasn't for that, I'd stay and work the claim for a while, myself. As it is, I can't stay that long."

Fallon turned on him, suddenly aware. "You're on the dodge!"

"Maybe."

Through it all, the girl sat quiet, numbed by the shock of her father's death and only vaguely aware these men were bartering her future. Sam looked trapped. He was polishing the same glass for the third time, his face pale and perspiring. But what could he do? What could any one man do? His one possible ally had failed him.

"You hurry," Red told them. "My information is for sale."

At that the girl looked up. "And you said you were my friend!" she said bitterly. "You're as bad as they are!"

Red shrugged. "Worse, in some ways. Sure, I'm your friend. I won't see you hurt or abused, but, lady, fifteen thousand is a lot of money! Your father refused a million for that claim."

"Stay here," Fallon said suddenly. "I'll go."

"No, you stay here," Porter interrupted. "I'll talk to him." He turned and went out of the door.

Clanahan glanced at the bartender. "Have the cook pack me some grub." He tossed a couple of silver dollars on the bar, and as the bartender reached for them, Red spread out two of his fingers, indicating two lunches. Only Sam could see the signal. He picked up the money and went back to the kitchen.

Shorty Taber crossed to the bar. His lips were swollen. Although the bleeding had stopped, his shirt was spotted with blood and his mouth split and bruised. He took a drink and then swore as the liquor bit sharply at the raw cuts. He glared viciously at Clanahan, who studiously ignored him.

Red picked up his glass and walked to the girl's table, never turning his back to the room. He sat down abruptly and said under cover of the movement: "Everything's all right. Main thing is to get you out of here."

Her eyes were cold. "After you've all robbed me? And murdered my father?" Her lips trembled.

Hastily, he said, "He was all right at the end, ma'am. He really was. Passed away, calm and serene."

Silence hung in the room and Red felt his own weariness creeping up on him. It seemed a long time since he had slept. The chase had been long and he had spent endless hours in the saddle. His head nodded, then jerked and his eyes were open. Shorty Taber was staring at him, his eyes gleaming with malice.

Red Clanahan turned to the girl. "I'm dead from sleep. When you hear a horse, wake me. Don't let them come near me. If they start to edge nearer, push me."

Almost at once, his head was over on the table on his arms. Elaine McClary sat very still, her hands on the table before her. Carefully, she kept her mind from any thought of her father. She dared not give way to grief. For the first time she began to be aware of her situation.

She had used almost her last money to get here to meet her father after his letter about the rich strike. She had not worried, because he had told her he had become a rich man. There was no one to whom she could now turn. She was alone. She was stranded. The one thing of value her father had managed to acquire was the claim and she had no idea where it was. Apparently nobody knew but the big red-headed man beside her.

She glared at him, seeing the rusty red curls

around his ears, the great leonine head, the massive shoulders. She had never seen any man with so much sheer physical power and strength. The size of his biceps was enormous to her eyes, and she remembered, with a queer little start, those cold green-gray eyes. Yet, had they been so cold?

A board creaked and her head turned swiftly. Taber was moving toward them. "Stay back," she said, "or I'll wake him."

Ebb Fallon looked up. "Shorty!" he snapped angrily. "Stay away from there! If anything happens to him, where do we stand?"

Taber turned with angry impatience and went back to the bar. "You weren't the one he hit," he said sullenly.

"Take your time," Fallon said. "This show ain't over yet."

Minutes went slowly by, and the big man beside her slept heavily. Several times he sighed and muttered in his sleep, and what she could see of his face was curiously relaxed and peaceful. His sun-faded shirt smelled of old sweat and dust, and now that she was closer to him, she could sense the utter and appalling weariness of the man. The dust of travel was on him, and he must have come far.

"Look, ma'am." Fallon seated himself at a nearby table and spoke softly, reasonably.

"Maybe we've gone at this all wrong. I admit we want that claim, but maybe we can make a dicker, you and us. Maybe we can do business. Now the way things shape up, you'll get nothin' for that claim. You could use money, I bet. You make a deal with us, and you won't lose it. You sell us your interest and we'll give you five hundred dollars."

"That claim is worth a million or more," she answered. "Father refused that for it, he said."

"But you don't know where it is. Think of that. According to law, you have to do assessment work on a claim; so much every year to hold it. Well, if you don't do your work, the claim is lost, anyway. How can you do it if you don't know where it is?"

Elaine shifted a little in her chair. All this was true, and it had already fled through her mind. She was so helpless. If there were only— If she could talk to Sam!

"I'll have to think about it," she said. "But what can I do?"

"Sign a bill of sale on that claim, and get the big hombre's gun. You're right beside it. All you have to do is take it. That hombre's an outlaw, anyway, ma'am. He'll sell you out."

But they had murdered her father! She

191

couldn't forget that. They had not even troubled to deny it.

Her eyes lifted and she saw Sam give her a faint negative shake of the head. "I'll think about it," she stalled.

If she took his gun, what then? They would kill this man as they had her father. Did that matter to her? Suddenly, she remembered! This big, lonely man beside her, this very tired big man, he had trusted her. He had asked her to help. Then, like a tired boy he had put down his head and slept among a bunch of murderers, trusting to her to warn him.

How soon would the mysterious boss be back? How far had Porter to go? How much time did she have?

Suppose *she* had the gun? Then she would be in a bargaining position herself! They would have to listen to her. But could she force the big man to talk? She knew that would be impossible for her. But not, she thought then, impossible for these other men. She read correctly the bitter hatred in Taber's eyes.

Frightened and alone, she sat in the lonely stage station and watched the hard, strange faces of these men she had never seen until scarcely an hour before. Now these strangers suddenly meant life and death to her.

She looked down at her hands, listening to

the bartender put down a glass on the back bar and take up another. Then she heard a faint drumming of horses' hoofs, and suddenly—why she would never know—she sprang to her feet, drawing the big red-headed man's gun as she did so and stepping back quickly.

Almost as suddenly, and catlike, wide-awake where a second before he had been sleeping, the big man was back against the wall. He stared at her, then around the room. "Give me that gun!" he said hoarsely.

"No."

Shorty Taber laughed suddenly, triumphantly. "How do you like it this way, Big Boy? Now look who's in the saddle!"

"Let me have the gun, ma'am," Fallon said reasonably. "I'll take it now."

She stepped back again. "No. Don't any of you come near me."

Her eyes caught the shocked horror in the bartender's eyes and doubt came to her. Had she done wrong? Should she have awakened the big man? She heard the horses draw up, heard two men dismount.

Porter entered, then another man—a big, wide-faced man with a tawny, drooping mustache and small, cunning blue eyes. He took in the tableau with a quick glance, then smiled.

193

His eyes went slowly to Clanahan. "Well, friend, looks like you weren't in such a good spot to bargain. Do you know where that claim is?"

"I sure do," Red snapped. Out of the corner of his mouth, he said to the girl: "Give me that gun, you little fool!"

"If she does, I'll shoot her," Taber said. "I never shot a woman yet, but so help me, I will. I'll shoot her, and then you."

"Shootin' a woman would be about your speed, Shorty." Red's tone was contemptuous. "Ever tackle a full-growed man?"

Shorty's nostrils flared and he swung his gun. "By the—"

"*Taber!*" The big man with the tawny mustache took a step forward. "You shoot and I'll kill you myself! Don't be a fool!"

There was a short, taut silence. "Now, Red," the big man said quietly, "we can do business. Looks to me like you're on the dodge. I saw your horse out there. A mighty fast horse, and it's come far and hard. I know that horse. It's from the Ruidoso, over in Lincoln County. Unless you knew that outfit well, you'd never have it. And if they let you have it, you're an outlaw."

"So?"

Red Clanahan stood very still, his big feet

194

apart, his eyes wary and alert. Like a photo-graph, that room with every chair, table, and man was in his mind.

"So we can do business," the tawny-mustached man said. "Tell me where that claim is and I'll give you a thousand dollars."

Red chuckled. "You foolin'?"

"You better." The newcomer was casual. "If you don't, you'll never get out of here alive. Nor will the girl."

They faced Red and the girl, who were seven or eight feet apart. Fallon was closest to her. Porter and the boys were nearest to Red.

"And you'd lose a million dollars." Red grinned tightly. "You make me smile. How many men are crawlin' over these hills now, lookin' for lost mines? How many will always be doin' it? Mister, you know and I know there's nothin' so lost as a lost mine. Gold once found is mighty shy about bein' found again. If you kill me, you haven't one chance in a million of findin' that gold."

"We could make him talk," Shorty suggested.

Red Clanahan laughed. "You think so? You little coyote, you couldn't make a ten-year-old kid talk. The Apaches worked on me for two days once, and I'm still here."

The boss eyed him. "Who are you, Red? Seems I ought to know you."

"You wouldn't, only by hearsay. I run with the lobos, not with coyotes."

The boss seemed to tighten and his eyes thinned down. "You use that word mighty free. Suppose we work on the girl? I wonder how fast you'd talk then?"

Red Clanahan shrugged. "How would that hurt me? She's a pretty kid, but I never saw her before she walked in here. She's nothing in my life. You torture her and all you'd get would be the trouble of it. You'd be surprised how I could bear up under other people's trouble."

"He ain't as tough as he looks," Taber said. "Let's work on the girl."

"No," the boss said, "I don't—" His voice broke off. Some of Red's relief must have shown in his eyes, for the boss suddenly changed his mind. "Why, yes, Shorty, I think we will. You take—"

The girl's gun seemed to waver, and Fallon grabbed for it. Instantly, the girl fired and Red Clanahan lunged.

He was cat-quick. With a bound he was half across the room. His shoulder struck Porter and knocked him careening into the boss, and both fell against the bar. Red's move had the immediate effect of turning all the fire away from the girl, shifting the center of battle. But his lunge carried him into a table and he fell over a chair. Yet as he hit the chair his big hand emerged from under his shirt with a second gun.

Fallon was struggling with the girl, and Red's first bullet caught Shorty in the midriff. Shorty took a step back, his eyes glazing. Guns exploded and flame stabbed. Red lunged to his feet, moving forward, swaying slightly, spotting his shots carefully, the acrid smell of gunpowder in his nostrils. Then suddenly the room was still.

Only the boss was on his feet and Fallon was stepping away from the girl, his hands lifted. The boss had blood trickling from his left shoulder. Shorty Taber was down, his eyes wide and empty.

Porter was slumped against the bar, a gun beside his hand, the front of his vest dark with blood, which was forming a pool under him.

Red moved swiftly and gathered up his second gun from where it had fallen. "Fifteen thousand, boss," he said quietly, "and I'll tell you what I know. I'll give you the map the girl's father drew for me." Red Clanahan holstered one gun. "Act fast," he said. "I haven't much time."

Sam looked at the boss. "You want me to get it out of the safe, Johnson?"

Johnson's voice was hoarse. He clutched his bloody shoulder. "Yeah." Then he begged. "Let me get my shoulder fixed. I'll bleed to death."

"Afterwards." Clanahan watched Sam go to the safe. "Johnson own this place, Sam?"

"Uh-huh."

"Looks like you're through here, then."

"You're tellin' me?" Sam brought two sacks to the counter. "They'd kill me after this."

"Then go saddle two horses. One for yourself and one for the lady."

"Miss," Clanahan gestured to her, "write him out a bill of sale to the claim designated on that map."

"But—" Elaine started a protest, then stifled it at Red's sudden impatience.

"Hurry!" he said angrily. "Do what I tell you!"

Red Clanahan saw Sam come around the building with the saddled horses, and yelled at him: "Tie Fallon," he said. "But let Johnson alone. By the time he gets Fallon loose and that shoulder fixed, we'll be too far off. And if he follows, we'll kill him."

Johnson took the map and the bill of sale, smiling suddenly. "Maybe it was worth a bullet-shot shoulder,'' he said. ''That's a rich claim.''

Sam picked up the gold and sacked it into the saddle bags. Then he picked up the lunch he had packed earlier, and two hastily filled canteens.

In the saddle, Red said hoarsely, ''Ride fast now! Get out of sight!''

Elaine glanced at him and was shocked by the sudden pallor of his face. ''You! You're hurt!'' she cried.

His wide face creased in a grin. ''Sure! But I didn't dare let those hombres guess it. Keep goin' a few miles. I can stick it.''

Beside a stream they paused and bandaged his wound. It was a deep gouge in the side, from which he had bled freely. He watched the girl work over it with quick, sure fingers.

''You'd do to take along, ma'am. You're sure handy.''

''I worked for a doctor.''

Back in the saddle, they switched off the trail and headed up through the timber.

Sam rode beside them, saying nothing. His round face was solemn.

''By the way,'' Red said, ''I better tell you. I looked at your dad's claim. And he was wrong, ma'am. It wasn't worth a million. It wasn't worth scarcely anything.''

Shocked, she looked around at him. "What do you mean?"

"Your dad struck a pocket of free gold. It was richer than all get-out, but your dad was no minin' man. There ain't a thousand dollars left in that pocket."

"Then—"

"Then if you'd kept it, you'd have had nothing but hard work and nothin' more. You got fifteen thousand."

"But I thought—"

Red chuckled. "Ma'am," he said, "I never stole from no woman. I just figured those hombres wanted that claim so bad, they should have it."

———

Cresting the divide, two days later, they saw the smoke of a far-off town. Red Clanahan drew up. "I leave you here. My trail," he pointed north, "goes that way. You take her to town, will you, Sam?"

The older man nodded. "Where are you headed, Red? The Roost?"

Clanahan glanced at him, wry humor in his eyes.

"Yeah. You know me?"

"Sure. I seen you once before, in Tascosa."

Clanahan glanced briefly at the girl. "Take

it easy with that money, ma'am." He lifted a hand. "So long."

The flanks of the horse gleamed black a time or two among the trees.

Elaine stared after him, her eyes wide and tear-filled.

"He—he is a good man, isn't he?" she said softly.

"Yeah, a real good man," Sam answered.

"What did you mean? The Roost?"

Sam rode on in silence; then he said, "Robber's Roost, ma'am. It's a hangout for outlaws up in the Utah canyon country. The way he rode will take him there."

"You knew him?"

"By sight, ma'am. His name's Red Clanahan, and they say he's killed nineteen men. It's said that he is a real badman."

"A good badman," she said, and looked again at where the horse had vanished in the trees. Once, far on a blue-misted ridge she thought she saw movement, a rider outlined briefly on the horizon. And then it was gone.

She might have been mistaken.

Showdown
on the Tumbling T

Author's Note

A man who was a gunfighter was simply a man who was good with a gun. His skill was usually the result of very steady nerves, very good reactions, and good coordination. A man might have had no intention of being a gunfighter at all, but then he got into a disagreement with somebody, and because of his ability, he was faster with a gun and he won. After he won two or three times he had a reputation as a gunfighter, whether he wanted it or not.

Very few gunfighters wanted to be known as such. The notion that a man went around trying to outdraw other people in order to build a big reputation seldom ever happened, unless they were either very young boys or somebody who was a psychopathic case.

Guns were dangerous and these men knew it. They carried guns because they were a tool of their living. You had to have them for many reasons aside from just wanting to shoot somebody else.

Chapter I
Death Trap

Under the slate-gray sky the distant mountains were like a heap of rusty scrap iron thrown helter-skelter along the far horizon. Nearby, the desert was the color of pink salmon and scattered with the gray of sagebrush and a few huddles of disconsolate greasewood. The only spot of green anywhere in sight was the sharp, strong green of tall pines in a notch of the rust-red mountains.

That was the place I'd come from Texas to find, the place where I was to hole up until Hugh Taylor could send word for me. It was something to have a friend like Hugh, someone to give you a hand up when the going was rough. When I had returned from Mexico to find myself a fugitive from justice, he had been the only one to offer help.

A few scattered drops of rain pounded dust from the desert. I dug into my pack for my slicker. By the time I had it on the rain was coming down in a steady downpour that looked fair to last the night through as well as the afternoon.

Rowdy, my big black, was beginning to feel the hard going of the past weeks. It was the only time I had ever seen the big horse even close to weariness, and it was no wonder. We had come out of Dimmit County, Texas, to the Apache country of central Arizona, and the trails had been rough.

The red rocks of the mountains began to take on form and line, and I could see the raw cancers of washes that ate into the face of the plain, and the deep scars of canyons. Here and there lines of gray or green climbed the creases in the rock, evidence of underlying water or frequent rains among the high peaks.

The trail curved north, skirting the mountains toward the sentinel pines. "Ride right to the Tin Cup ranch," Hugh Taylor had said, "and when you get there, ask for Bill Keys. He'll be in charge, and he'll fix you up until this blows over. I'm sure I can get you cleared in a short time."

The mountains cracked wide open on my left and the trail turned up a slope between the pines. Blue gentians carpeted both sides of the road and crept back under the trees in a solid mass of almost sky-blue. The trail was faint, and apparently used very little, but there were tracks made by two riders and I watched them curiously. The tracks were fresh and they were headed into the Tin Cup canyon.

You can bet I had my eyes open, for even so far away from anyone that knew me there might be danger, and a man on the dodge learns to be careful.

Then I heard a shot.

It rapped out sharp and clear and final, bringing my head up with a jerk and my hand down to the stock of my Winchester. My rifle rode in a scabbard that canted back so that the stock almost touched my right thigh, and I could draw that rifle almost as fast as a man could draw a six-gun.

Rowdy heard that shot, too, and Rowdy knew what shooting could mean. He skirted the rocks that partially barred the way into the Tin Cup, and I looked down into a little valley with a stone barn and stone house, two corrals, and two riderless horses.

Then I saw the men. The air was sharp and clear, and they were only a couple of hundred yards off. There were three of them, and one was lying on the ground. The man who stood over the body looked up and yelled at the other one near the corner of the house. "No, it ain't him!" And then they both saw me.

Panic must have hit them both, but one of them made a break for his horse while the other swung his hand down for his gun. Honest men don't start shooting when a stranger rides up; so as his six-gun lifted, my rifle cleared the boot. He fired, but I wasn't worried. He was much too far away.

He made a dive for his horse and I held my fire. As he settled in the saddle I squeezed off my shot. He jerked like he was hit and I saw the gun fall from his hand into the rocks, and then they were taking out of there, but fast. They wanted no part of my shooting.

Rowdy wasn't gun-shy. With me in the saddle he had no cause to be, after all we had been through down Mexico way. That was a part of my life I never talked about much, and even Hugh, who was my best friend, knew nothing about it. To him I was still the quiet kid he had seen grow up on our uncle's ranch, the XY.

Rowdy was in no shape for a chase, so I let the riders go and swung down beside the old man and felt of his pulse. That was mostly a matter of form. No man with that last bullet hole where he had it was going to be alive. The first shot was a bit high, and I could see there had been some interval, for the blood around the first wound was coagulated.

A horse's hoof clicked on stone and I turned

with my hands spread. You don't pull anything fancy when four men are looking down rifles at you.

"What did you kill him for?" The speaker was a squat, broad-chested man with a square red face and gimlet eyes. He looked tough as a winter in the mountains, and at least two of the riders with him looked fit to side with the devil on a ride through hell.

"Don't jump your fences, pardner," I told him, pretty chilly. "I didn't shoot this gent. When I rode into the Cup two hombres were standing here, one right over him. They took a shot at me, then lit out, ridin' up the valley as I came in."

"We heard shootin'," the square-faced man replied. "He's dead an' you're here."

My eyes went over them, sizing them up. Nobody needed to burn any brands on this hide for me. Here I was on the dodge from one killing of which I wasn't guilty, and now I'd run smack-dab into another. Nobody had seen those other riders but me, so what happened now depended a whole lot on just who and what these men were.

At first glance I could see there was only one man of the four who would give anybody a break. He was a young fellow with brown eyes and dark hair, and a careful look in his eyes.

He looked smart and he looked honest, although a man can be fooled on both counts.

The square-built man who had done the talking seemed to be the big gee. "Who are you, anyway?" he demanded. "What brings you here?"

Something in the way he asked that question let me get downwind of an idea. I decided to tell this hombre nothing, least of all that I was Wat Bell. "Why, they call me the Papago Kid, and I'm from down Sonora way.

"As for what brings me here, it was this black horse brought me, and the trail through the pines. A lot of trails have brought me a lot of places, and"—I added this with some meaning—"when I wanted to ride out, nobody stopped me."

His eyes sharpened down and his lips thinned out. I could see the old devil coming up in his eyes. This man was not one you could push far. He figured he was some salty, and he had no liking for being called up to the mark by any casual drifter. However, there was a funny little frown came into his eyes when I mentioned my name; and somehow the idea was there, full size and ready for branding, that he had expected another name. That feeling was so strong in me that it started me thinking about a lot of things.

Sometimes a man rides trails and reads sign so long that he develops an instinct for things. There was the strong smell of trouble in my nostrils now, and for some reason I knew that I'd made a good bet when I told him I was the Papago Kid. The funny part of it was that if he could find a way to check back down the Sonora trail, he'd find out I hadn't lied. A man sometimes can have two names that take separate trails, and if I was young Wat Bell in Dimmit County, Texas, I was also the Papago Kid down in Sonora.

"Lynch," the young fellow interrupted, "let's get in out of this rain, and get the body in, too. I liked old Tom Ludlow, and I don't like his body lying around like this." Then he added, "We can talk just as well over some coffee, anyway."

Lynch hesitated, still not liking me, and itching for gunplay. "All right," he agreed, and turning to the other riders, a fat-faced man and a tall, stoop-shouldered rider, he added, "you two pick Ludlow's body up and cart it out to the stable. Cover it with a blanket and then come on in. Better put the horses in, too." He looked at the tall man. "Don't leave anything undone, Bill," he added.

When I heard the tall man called Bill a faint suspicion stirred in me, but I didn't look up.

213

When I did, the fat man answered my question for me without any talking from me. "You take his feet, Keys. I'll get his shoulders."

Lynch turned abruptly toward the door of the stone house and I followed with the young fellow behind me. Inside, Lynch got out of his slicker and I got a shock. He was wearing a sheriff's badge on his vest.

"The coffee was your idea, Dolliver," Lynch suggested. "Want to start it?"

Dolliver nodded, and I knew he had seen my reaction to that badge and was curious about it. He turned toward the shelves and began taking things down as if he knew the place. In the meantime I was trying to scout my trail and read the sign of this situation I'd run into.

Hugh Taylor had told me to ride to the Tin Cup and ask for Bill Keys. Yet when I arrived here, there was a dead man on the ground who isn't Bill Keys but is apparently the owner of the place. Meanwhile, Keys appears to be riding for the sheriff, and with what reason I had no idea.

It was a neat little house, tidy as an old maid's boudoir, and the smell of coffee that soon filled the room gave it a cozy, homelike feel. The fireplace was big enough, and all the cooking utensils were bright and clean. A blanket over a door curtained off an inner room.

Lynch dropped astride a chair and began to build a smoke. He had a bullet head covered with tight ringlets and a mustache that drooped in contrast. Slinging my hat on a hook, I hung up my own slicker and dropped into another chair. Lynch saw my two guns and his face chilled a little. Something about me disturbed him, and I decided it was partly the guns—the fact that I was wearing them, not that he feared them.

"You call yourself the Papago Kid?" Lynch's question was sharp.

My eyes held his and I knew Sheriff Lynch and I were not going to be friends. He was distinctly on the prod, but he was digging for something, too. I was beginning to wonder if I didn't know what it was he wanted. "I've been called that," I said, "and I like the name. You can use it."

"Did you get a good look at those two riders who lit out of here? The two you said you saw?"

"I did see them. No, the look I got wasn't too good. One of them legged it for his bronc and the other grabbed iron. Naturally, with a man drawing a gun on me, even at that distance, I wasn't wasting any time looking him over."

"How many shots did you hear?"

"One."

Dolliver turned around from the coffee. "I heard three."

"That's right," I agreed. "One shot apparently killed the old man. Then I rounded into sight and one of these hombres took a shot at me. I shot back." I hitched my chair back a little. "However, as you no doubt saw, the old man was shot twice. I figure he was wounded some place away from the ranch, then trailed down by the killers, who finished the job."

"What gives you that idea?" Lynch demanded

"If you noticed, Sheriff," I said, "the rain hadn't washed out the old man's tracks. Those tracks came from toward the corrals, and even from where I stood I could see the old man had fallen down twice on that little slope, and there were blood spots on his clothes."

It was obvious enough that the sheriff had seen nothing of the kind, and he studied me carefully. I was doing some thinking on my own hook. The reason the sheriff hadn't seen those tracks was because all his attention had been centered on me.

Dolliver, whose attitude I liked, brought the coffee up to the table and filled our cups. He was a clean-cut youngster and no fool.

The door opened then and Bill Keys came in with his fat friend. They knocked the rain from their hats and shed their slickers, both of them looking me over while they were doing it. Dolliver filled cups for them and they found chairs and sat down.

It struck me as faintly curious that Sheriff Lynch was making no effort to trail the men I had mentioned, nor to see if there were tracks to back up my story. I wondered what Dolliver thought of that, and was glad that he was with us. This was new country for me, and I was definitely in a bad spot, and unless the breaks came my way I'd soon have the choice of shooting my way out or I'd find myself looking into my past through the leaves of a cottonwood with the loop end of a rope around my neck.

"You ever been in this country before?" Lynch demanded.

"Never. When I left my home in California, I crossed Arizona down close to Yuma and went into Mexico."

"How'd you happen to find this place? It ain't the easiest valley to find." He stared at me suspiciously, his eyes trying to pry behind my guileless eyes. I was wearing my most innocent face, carefully saved for just such emergencies.

"Did you ever cross that desert behind here?" I asked. "The only spot of green a man can see is right here. Naturally, I headed for the pines.

Figured there might be people where there was water.''

That was simple enough even for him, and he mulled over it a little. ''You said you came from California? You sound like a Texan to me.''

''Hell,'' I grinned cheerfully, ''it's no wonder! On the last spread I rode for down Mexico way there were eight Texans. My folks spoke Spanish around home,'' I lied, ''so when I talked English with that Texas outfit, naturally I picked up their lingo.''

The story was plausible enough, but Lynch didn't like it. He didn't get a chance to ask any more questions for a minute, as I beat him to it. ''What's up, Sheriff?'' I asked. ''Is this a posse? And if it is, why pick on me?''

Lynch didn't like that, and he didn't like me. ''Huntin' a Texas outlaw supposed to be headed this way,'' he said, grudgingly, ''a murderer named Wat Bell. We got word he was headed west so we're cuttin' all the trails.''

''Bad weather to be riding,'' I sympathized, ''unless you're on a red-hot trail. Is this Bell a bad hombre? Will it take four of you?''

Dolliver's eyes were shrewd and smiling. ''I'm not one of them,'' he told me. ''I have a little ranch just over the mountain from here, and joined these boys back in the pines when they headed this way. My ranch is the Tumbling T.''

Chapter II
Puzzle on the Tumbling T

Lynch ended his questions and devoted himself to his coffee. From the desultory conversation that followed while Lynch mulled things over, I learned that the dead man, old Tom Ludlow, had owned the Tin Cup, and had no enemies that anybody knew. Win Dolliver was his nearest neighbor, and liked the old man very much, as had his sister, Maggie Dolliver.

The nearest town was Latigo, where Sheriff Ross Lynch had his office. The fat rider was Gene Bates, but nothing more was said about Wat Bell or what made the sheriff so sure he could find him that he started out on a rainy day. Knowing the uncertainties of travel in the West, and the liking of sheriffs for swivel chairs, I had a hunch that somebody had tipped the sheriff. It was less than reasonable to suppose he would start out with two men in bad weather merely on the chance that the man he sought was coming to Arizona.

Lynch looked up suddenly. ''We'll be ridin'

219

on into Latigo,'' he said, ''and I reckon you'd better come along.''

''Are you arresting me?''

His blue eyes turned mean again. He didn't like me even a little bit. ''Not necessarily,'' he said, ''but we'll be wantin' to ask you questions, an' we'll be gettin' answers.''

''Look, my friend.'' I leaned forward just a little, and having my hands on my hips as I did, the move put my gun butts practically in my palms. ''I'm not planning to get stuck for something somebody else did. You rode down here and for some reason assumed I was the guilty man. Anyway, you're all set on taking me in.

''You made no effort, and I'll leave it to Dolliver here, to check my story. You've sat here while the rain washed or partly washed those tracks away. You made no effort to get after those killers.

''You claim you're hunting some killer named Wat Bell, yet when you got here all the ambition seemed to leave you. Mr. Sheriff, I'm not your man. I didn't kill Tom Ludlow. I never saw him before. I have all the money I need, and a better horse than any of you ride. Ludlow had nothing at all that I could want. The only shot I've fired was from my rifle, and Ludlow was shot with a pistol, and that last one was fairly close up.''

Lynch looked ugly. "I know what I'm doin'!" he stated flatly. "I've got my reasons!"

This looked like a good time to let them in on something. How anxious they were for gunplay, I didn't know. I did know that I stood a much better chance right here than on the trail. I'd a sudden hunch that might be haywire as could be, but it might be correct. I'd a hunch Lynch had been told Wat Bell was coming right to the Tin Cup. I'd a further hunch that Wat Bell was not supposed to leave this ranch alive, and also that while Lynch now had doubts that I was Wat Bell, he was very apt to gun me down once I was on the road with the three of them.

"All right!" I said, "You've got your reasons! Well, I have mine for not going into Latigo with you! I don't wear two guns just for fun, and if those two shots had been fired at Ludlow by me he'd never have come back to this ranch. If you want to call my bluff and see whether I savvy guns or not, just buy chips in my game and you'll see!"

He was madder right then than a wildcat in a swarm of bees, but he wasn't very happy about the spot he was in. Ross Lynch was not yellow, not by a jugful, but I knew there were several things about this setup he didn't like. The presence of Win Dolliver, whom I now knew had joined him by accident, was one of them. Another was the fact that I said I was the Papago Kid. That name meant nothing to him. But if, as I now believed, he had been tipped off that Wat Bell was coming to this ranch, then I had confused the issue enough so that he wasn't sure who I was.

Also, he was no fool. He had seen those two guns, and the guns had seen use. If we cut our dogs loose in this cabin, somebody was going to get hurt besides me. Nobody knew that better than Lynch.

Dolliver smoothed things over. He was a smart hombre, that one. "There's something to what he says, Ross. After all, why should we suspect him? It could just as easily have been me who found Ludlow. I was headed this way when I met you boys.

"We should have looked for those tracks, too. I'm honest to say that I never thought of it." He turned to me. "Did you hit the man you shot at?"

"Burned him, I think. His horse was moving. I held my fire, but it was the best chance I had." Right then I decided to say nothing about the gun the rider had dropped, but to have a look the first chance I got. That gun might be a clue that would help me ferret out the answer to this deal.

Lynch was getting ready to say something,

and I was sure I wouldn't like it. Dolliver interrupted. "Look, Ross," he said quietly, "don't blame the Kid here for being on the prod. You can't blame him, riding into a deal like this. He certainly could have no reason to shoot Ludlow. Let him come on over to my place with me. I can use a hand for a few days, and when you want to see him, ride over. That will clear this situation up, and I think Papago will agree to work for me. I'll pay him top hand's wages."

"That's good for me," I agreed. "I'm not hunting trouble. I'll do all I can to find that killer, and if you want, I'll try to trail those men for you. I've ridden trails before," I added, and I pointed this one right at Lynch, "and found out right where they ended."

Lynch didn't like it, but no more than any other man did he have a stomach for gunplay in that close quarters. The presence of Win Dolliver was a big help, and allowed him a chance to back out and save face.

The same questions kept coming into my mind. How had they learned Wat Bell was headed this way? Why had Hugh Taylor told me to ask for Bill Keys on the Tin Cup when it was owned by Ludlow? Who had killed the old man, and why?

Bill Keys was another puzzle. Taylor had

said the man could be trusted, but he didn't size up right to me. How good a description did he have of me? Or did he have one at all? Hugh might not have known him so well, and could have been mistaken in trusting him. For one, I was doing no talking until I understood the lay of the land.

Something else had come into my mind that somehow I'd never thought of before. When Hugh Taylor had met me that night and told me of my uncle's murder, and that I was wanted for it, I had thought of little else. True, I had left town rather suddenly after a quarrel with old Tom Bell, but that he had been murdered on the night I left for Mexico, I'd had no idea until then. Hugh had showed me the reward poster, but had assured me that he didn't believe me guilty. He had investigators working on the crime, and advised me to go away and stay in hiding until he sent for me.

My mind was full of questions. Had my uncle left a will? And to whom had he left two hundred thousand acres of his ranch? And who *had* killed him?

Bill Keys got up and turned toward the door and my eyes dropped to his gun, absently noting that a chip had been broken from the bone handle, and the break looked recent. Sheriff Ross Lynch and Bates followed him out, and then Dolliver and I. When he rode around the corner of the house, Keys was saddling a horse with which to carry the body into town.

Once around the house, I slid from the saddle and scrambled into the rocks. A hasty look showed me only one thing. The gun was gone!

Win Dolliver looked at me curiously, but said nothing until we were well along the trail to the Tumbling T. It was just six miles, and Dolliver talked pleasantly and easily of the country, the cattle, and the rain. Ludlow had been running only about six hundred head, while he had four times that many. Keys and Bates, holding a ranch in partnership, ran a few head over west.

When we were in sight of his own ranch, Win turned. "Did you get a good look at those riders? Enough to know them again?"

"No," I admitted, realizing this was the first pointed question he had asked, and wondering what was behind it, "but one of them lost a gun back there. When I looked it was gone."

"Maybe you just didn't find it?"

"No, I saw where it had been. There was a boot track near it."

We didn't say anything more right then because the door opened and a girl stepped out on

225

the porch and I forgot everything I had been thinking and all that had happened.

There is no description for a girl like that. It was simply that this was the girl I had been looking for all my life. It wasn't a matter of eyes nor hair, although hers were beautiful; it was simply that here she was, the girl that was meant for me. She was trimly shaped and neat, and there was quick laughter in her eyes, and there was interest and appraisal, too.

"Mag," Dolliver said, swinging down, "meet the Papago Kid. He's riding through the country and has had a little trouble with Ross Lynch."

"That's nothing against him on the T!" Maggie Dolliver replied with spirit. "You know what I think of Ross!"

Win chuckled. "Everybody should, after the way you told him off at the last Latigo dance! But what about Howie Taber?"

She flushed, and I didn't miss that. The name struck me, too. "Who did you say?" I asked.

"Taber. He is a partner of Lynch's in a ranch they have out here. At least Taber owns the ranch and Lynch runs the cows when he's not working at being sheriff. Pretty well off, Taber is. And he made quite a play for Maggie when he was out here last."

Maggie made better coffee than Win, I found, and her cookies were wonderful. I listened mostly, and answered a few random questions about Mexico. Then I started in, and asked my first question. "What about Keys? Who is he?"

"Keys?" The question puzzled Dolliver. "Frankly, I don't like the man. He ranches some with Bates, as I said, and he and Lynch are thicker than thieves. There's a story around that he ran with that horse-stealing outfit down in the Bradshaws, but I wouldn't know how true it is. He's also supposed to be something of a gun hawk. He has killed one man I know of—a drifter in Latigo."

Maggie looked at me curiously; then a thought seemed to occur to her and she turned to Win. "What I can't understand is why anyone would want to kill a nice old man like Uncle Tom Ludlow!"

"It was a mistake," I said, repeating what I had overheard when I rode up on the killers. "I think they were looking for someone else."

"But who?" Win puzzled. "And why?"

"I think," I said deliberately, "they were looking for me. I think they saw a rider at the expected place and shot him, then finished him off to prevent him talking when they found their mistake."

"But who was it they were after?" Maggie demanded.

"Me," I repeated dryly. "I think they wanted me."

Moreover, I told myself, if they had wished to kill me and had failed, they would surely try again. Had they been sure that I was Wat Bell rather than the Papago Kid, they would have insisted I go to town with them, and shot me, "trying to escape" on the way in. As it was, probably Win Dolliver's presence had saved me at first sight.

"Don't take what I said about working too seriously," Win volunteered, after a moment. "My main idea was to get you away from Lynch without a fight. He's tough, and he didn't like you. I could see that. Dangerous as he is, I think you've more to fear from Bill Keys."

Neither of them asked me any questions, nor why I believed it had been me the killers wanted. Whatever their reason for inviting me here, and I was convinced there was a reason, they asked no questions and offered no information.

Chapter III
Papago Makes a Hand

Nevertheless, I was up at daybreak with the hands, ate breakfast with them and with Win, and rode out to work with them. Later in the morning when Maggie came out to join us, I overheard him tell her, "Whatever else he may be, Mag, he's a hand. He's done more work than any two of the regular boys."

Maybe it was because these cedar brakes were a pipe after brush-popping down in the Big Bend, where I had worked two years, but I did get a lot done. And maybe because it was good to have a rope in my hands and a cow by the tail instead of only a gun. Yet all the time I worked, my mind was busy, and it didn't like what seemed to be truth.

A lot of loose ends were beginning to find their way to a common point, and I had begun to see that in skipping out of Texas I had made a big mistake. Hugh Taylor, aside from being my cousin, was also my friend, or so I had believed. From anyone but him I would never have taken the advice he had given.

Hugh Taylor had run off from the ranch where we were growing up when he was sixteen, and returned again after four years. After being around a year, he took off again, and returned some months later with money and a silver-mounted saddle. He was bigger than I, and rugged. He was also two years older. A top hand at anything he did, he stood high in my uncle's favor.

Yet I'd worked on at the ranch, never leaving, punching cows, mending fence, riding herd. I had taken two herds north over the trail, and I'd had a gunfight in Abilene, and killed my man. I wasn't proud of that, and as only a few of the trail hands returned, and they promised not to talk, nobody around the XY knew. Later, when I was down in the Big Bend with a bunch of cattle, we had trouble with Mexican bandits, and I went into their camp, brought back some stolen horses, and did it without firing a shot.

Finally, when I was twenty-four, Uncle Tom and I had a big argument, and I got mad and lit out for Mexico. Crossing the Border, I didn't want to be known as Uncle Tom Bell's nephew, so I called myself the Papago Kid. Riding through Coahuila to Durango, I had several fights, and then, moving up into Sonora, I tied up with old Valverdes and protected his ranch against bandits. While there I had two more gunfights, one with a Mexican gunman, the other with an American.

Then, after being away two years, I had returned across the Border and the first person I'd met was Hugh. At the time it seemed a stroke of luck, and I remember how startled he was to see me.

"You here, Wat?" he had exclaimed. "Don't you know you're wanted for murder?"

That got me, and in reply to my heated questions, he told me that the night after our quarrel Uncle Tom had been shot and killed, that I was sought as the killer, but a story had returned to the XY that I had been killed by bandits in Mexico.

"Your best bet is to get out of here," he told me. "Ride west to Arizona. I've some friends out there, and in the meantime I'll do what I can to straighten this up."

So my uncle was dead, and they believed I had killed him. I hadn't, but somebody else had, and who was that somebody? Also, what kind of a deal had Hugh sent me into at the Tin Cup? I arrive to find a man murdered, and the sheriff hunting a "Texas outlaw" known as Wat Bell—and knowing exactly where to find him and when.

That last didn't make sense until I began to remember my last stop before getting there. It had been in Lincoln, New Mexico, and I had stopped there with a friend of Hugh Taylor's. Now if that friend had wired Sheriff Lynch, and Lynch had done a little figuring as to miles a day, it would not be too hard to arrive at the day of my arrival at the Tin Cup—a sufficiently secluded spot for murder.

Uncle Tom Bell had no relatives anyone knew of but Hugh and myself, so he would

231

naturally leave his two hundred thousand acres to us, and if one of us died, then the other would inherit everything. I didn't like to think that of Hugh, but he had been a little greedy, I remembered, even as a youngster.

A few discreet inquiries around proved that nobody had ever heard of Hugh Taylor, yet Taylor knew people here, and they knew him. I was still studying about that when Mag loped her pony over to where I sat my horse, watching the herd we'd bunched.

"Win tells me you're a hand!" she said, smiling at me. "I hope you decide to stay. He likes you, and it will be lonesome for him after I leave."

That hit me hard. I turned in my saddle. "After you leave? Then you're going away?"

She must have seen something in my face because hers suddenly changed and the smile went out of it. "I . . . I'm going to be married," she said quietly.

That was all. Neither of us had another thing to say right then. For me, she had said it all. If in all the world there was a girl for me, this was the one. I wanted her as I never had wanted anything. But I was just the Papago Kid, and a fugitive from the law.

What she was thinking I have no idea, but she didn't look happy. We just sat there watching the herd until it started to move. There were enough men to handle it and I made no move to follow.

"You're quiet," she said finally. "You don't say anything."

"What can I say?" I asked her honestly enough. "You've just said it all."

She didn't act mystified and want an explanation, for she knew as well as I what I meant and how I felt. She did finally say something, and it was so much what a lot of girls would have said that it enabled me to get my feet on the ground again. She said, "You've only known me a few hours."

"How long does it take? Is there a special time, or something? A special set of rules that says flatly a man has to know a girl three weeks, seventeen hours and nine minutes before he can fall in love with her? And another set that says she must know him six months, four hours and five minutes before she can admit she likes him?

"There isn't any time limit and there never has been," I told her. "To some people it comes quick, to others slow. With me it was the minute you walked out on the porch back there, and I rode into the yard. That's exactly when it was. The rest doesn't matter."

My voice wasn't a lover's voice. It was

pretty sharp and hard because I felt just that way. Then it hit me all of a sudden and I could see it plain as day. "Well, at least he didn't steal you!"

She looked up quickly, her eyes going wide with surprise. "Steal me? Who?"

"Hugh Taylor," I said.

"Who?" She looked puzzled and a little frightened. "What do you mean?"

"I mean Howie Taber—the one who was a friend of Lynch's, only his name is Hugh Taylor, and he's my cousin."

"Your cousin?" She was staring at me now, but there was not so much surprise in her eyes as I had expected. "What are you talking about?"

"I'm talking about a big blond and handsome man with broad shoulders and deep-set blue eyes, a man with a small scar on the point of his chin, who rides good horses and wears flashy clothes and handles a gun well. That's who I mean. A man who is my cousin but who could easily have called himself Howie Taber."

Her face was white now, but she was staring right through me. "And what is your name?" she demanded.

"I'm Wat Bell," I told her. "I am the man Lynch was looking for at the Tin Cup, and how did he know I'd be there? Only one man in all the world knew it, and that man was Hugh—who I thought was my best friend.''

''I don't believe that,'' she said. ''I don't believe any of it. You may know him, but you're an outlaw, masquerading under a false name. You've made all this up.''

''All right,'' I said, ''I made it up!'' With that I reined my horse around and started back for the T. If I had been riding Rowdy I'd never have gone back at all, but this was a cowhorse I'd borrowed, wanting to save the big black after his long trek across country.

There was only one thing in my mind then, to get Rowdy and hit the trail out of there, but fast. And where to? Back to Texas! To prove that I hadn't killed my uncle. To prove that I was no outlaw.

The cowhorse I was on was a good horse and he took me over the hill to the T at a fast lope, and I came up from behind the corrals and hit the dirt, and then stopped. Right there across the yard from me was Ross Lynch, and beside him was Gene Bates. Win Dolliver was on the step, and his face looked dark as death and just as solemn. Lynch stepped out toward me and stopped. ''Wat Bell!'' he said. ''I arrest you for murder!''

''Whose murder?'' I demanded.

''The murder of Tom Ludlow!'' he said.

Then he smiled. "There is a charge against you in Texas, but we'll hang you for this one!"

I was mad all the way through. My hands swinging at my sides, I looked at him. "Ross Lynch, I did not murder Ludlow, and you damn' well know it. You know it because you know who did! And I know! It was—!"

Gene Bates' hand swept down for a gun and so did Lynch. My own guns were coming up and I took a quick step forward and right and fired quickly—too quickly. My first bullet knocked the gun from the sheriff's hand, and I hadn't intended it that way. I wanted to kill him. The second one took Gene Bates right over the belt buckle.

Win Dolliver hadn't moved. He stood there on the steps, his eyes wide. But what he thought he wasn't saying. I don't know where Maggie was. On the bunkhouse steps were two of the boys and another one stood at the corral. He turned to his saddle pockets and dug out a box of .44s. "Catch!" he said simply, and tossed it.

"Thanks!" I caught the box in my left hand and backed toward the corral. Lynch was holding his numbed hand and staring at me.

"I'll kill you for this!" he said. "I'll kill you if it's the last thing I do!"

"If you do, it will be!" I told him. Astride

236

the cowpony, I looked at Win. "Thanks, Dolliver. You've been mighty square. Tom Ludlow was killed by Gene Bates and Bill Keys. That chip on the bone-handle of Keys' gun was broken off when it fell into the rocks, you know where!"

Then I reined my horse around and hit the trail at a fast run.

———

That pony had worked hard, but he was game. He stayed with that run until he hit timber, and then I slowed him down to a canter, and then to a walk. After that I began to Injun my trail. I took so many twists and turns I was dizzy, and I rode up and down several streams, across several shelves of rock and through some sand. And then I doubled back and headed for the Tin Cup.

My horse wouldn't go far and he needed rest. I needed food. There was food in the cabin, and every chance they wouldn't think of it right away. Also, it was within striking distance of the T, and I had no idea of leaving Rowdy. That big black horse meant a lot to me, and ever since old Valverdes gave him to me, I'd treated him like a child.

Now I was an outlaw, having resisted arrest, the first crime I'd committed. But if I could prove that Bates and Keys had killed Ludlow, and with the sheriff's knowledge, I'd be in the clear even on that. And it was something I intended to prove.

From the expression on Lynch's face I knew that shooting of mine had been a distinct shock. Hugh hadn't warned them about that simply because he didn't know. Hugh had always beaten me in shooting matches. That was before I went to Mexico. He had probably told Lynch I was only a fair shot. Well, the shooting that knocked the gun from his hand and drilled Bates had been good shooting, the kind he wouldn't be too anxious to tackle again.

By sundown I was bedded down in the pines watching the Tin Cup ranchhouse. All through the final hours of daylight I watched it and studied the trails. I wanted no traps laid for me, although I doubted if they would think of the Tin Cup right away.

It was well after midnight before I started down the trail to the ranch, and I took my horse only a short distance, then left him tied in the brush and cat-footed it down by myself, leaving my spurs on the horn of my saddle.

Nothing looked very good right then. I had killed Gene Bates and resisted arrest. Hugh Taylor, whom I'd considered my best friend, had tried to trap me into an ambush, and Maggie

Dolliver, the girl I wanted more than anything in life, was in love with Hugh. Right then I'd about as little to live for as any man, but I'd a lot of resentment—nor was I one to bow my head before the storm and ride off letting well enough alone.

When I did ride off it would be with my name clear, and also I would know and the world would know who had killed Uncle Tom Bell. Until then I had a job to do.

The warm sun of the late afternoon had baked the ground hard after the rain, and I moved carefully. The stone house was dark and still when I tried the door, and it eased open without a sound. Once inside I wasted no time, for while Win had been making coffee on the day of the killing, I had seen where the food was kept. Hastily, I reached for the coffee sack. It was almost empty!

Puzzled, for it had been nearly full when I last saw it, I reached for the beans, and they were gone. And then there was a whisper of movement behind me and I turned, palming my gun as I moved.

"Don't shoot!" The voice was low, but the very sound of it thrilled me so that I couldn't have squeezed a trigger if I'd wished. "The food is on the table, all packed."

"Mag! You did this . . . for me?" I couldn't

believe that, and moved around the table toward her. She had been in that inner room, waiting behind the blanket-covered door.

"Yes." The word was simple and honest. "I did it for you, and I've no idea whether I'm doing right or not. Maybe all they say about you is true. Maybe you did kill your uncle and maybe you did kill Tom Ludlow."

"You don't believe that?"

"No." She hesitated. "No, I don't believe I do. I know Ross Lynch, Wat—that is your name, isn't it? He has been mixed up in so many wrong things. It was the only fault I could find with Howie—that he trailed with Lynch and that devil, Bill Keys."

In the darkness I could not see her eyes, but suddenly my hands lifted to her shoulders. "Mag," I said softly, "I've got to ride out of here. Whatever else I do, I've got to clear myself, and I'm going to do it, an' if the trouble strays over on somebody else's range, I'm going to follow it there.

"I could go away now, taking the blame for Old Man Ludlow like they've already hung the blame on me for Uncle Tom, but I won't do it. I won't have you doubting me, even if I never see you again. Nor do I want folks to think I've killed Uncle Tom, after he did so much for me."

She didn't say anything for a moment, and with her arms all warm under my hands it was all I could do to keep from drawing her close. Finally, she spoke. "Do what you have to do, Wat. I know how you feel."

"But, Mag, suppose that somebody you— Well, I mean, suppose that when I find who did this killing, I find it was somebody close to you. What then?"

She looked up at me again. "Why, then, Wat, it would have to be that way. I guess I knew you felt like this, I knew who you believed was guilty, but I came here and got this food ready for you, sure that you'd come. I brought your horse, too, Wat. He's in the shadow by the stable."

"Rowdy?" My voice lifted, then lowered. "You did that? Oh, you darlin'! Now I'll feel like a man again! This pony, he tries hard and he's got a great heart, but he's not Rowdy."

"I knew how you felt about him." She drew back. "Now you'd better go. Ride out of here, and good luck, whatever you do, or whatever comes!"

Chapter IV
Horsethief Valley

That was just the way I left, with that pack over my shoulder, slipping out to find Rowdy, who

241

nudged me with his nose and stamped content-
edly. But I waited there until she was on her
horse and gone, and then I slid into the saddle
and headed for the hills. When I got to where
I'd left the pony, I tied the bridle reins up and
turned him loose, knowing he'd find his way
back to the T.

Already I'd had an idea. Bill Keys had
come from the Bradshaws, and that was where
I was heading, right for Horsethief Valley. There
had to be a tie-up there. Nor was I waiting until
morning. Rowdy was rested and ready for the
trail, and I took it, riding west across the mountains, skirting Latigo, and heading on west. On
the third night I camped at Badger Spring, up a
creek from the canyon of the Agua Fria, and
after a quick breakfast in the morning, crossed
the Bumblebee and Black Canyon and headed
up the Dead Cow. Skirting the peak on a bench
I cut down the mountainside into Horsethief
Canyon.

Western men knew the West, and it was no
wonder that even as far east as Dimmit County,
Texas, we knew about the horsethief trails that
cut through the country from Robber's Roost
and the Hole in the Wall to Mexico. This place
was only a way station, but from all I'd heard I
knew some of the crowd that trailed stolen
horses, and they were a hard bunch of men.

Rowdy had a feeling for trouble. The big black pricked his ears toward the ramshackle cluster of cabins and corrals that lay on the flat among the mountains. Nobody needed to tell me that we were not watched all the way down that trail, and when Rowdy drew up in front of the combination saloon and store that was the headquarters at Horsethief, a half-dozen men idled on the steps.

Across at the big barn a man sat on a bench with a Henry rifle across his knees, and another man whittled idly in front of a cabin even further along.

When I swung down I tied Rowdy to the rail and stepped up on the porch and dug out the makings. "Howdy," I offered.

A lean, hatchet-faced man, who looked the type to murder his mother-in-law, looked up. "Howdy."

Nobody said anything and when I'd built a smoke I offered the tobacco around, but nobody made a move to accept. A short, stocky rider with run-down heels on his boots squatted against the wall. He looked up at me, then nodded at Rowdy. "Quite a hoss. Looks like he could make miles."

"He made 'em to here." I looked at Shorty again. "Want a drink? I'll buy."

He got up with alacrity. "Never refused a

drink!'' he warned me. We pushed through the doors and bellied up to the bar. There was a smell of cured bacon, dry goods, and spices curiously intermingled. I glanced around the store, and sized up the fat man in the dirty shirt who bounced around to the bar side and made a casual swipe at the bar top with a rag.

''What'll it be, gents?''

Shorty chuckled. ''He says 'what'll it be' ever'time, an' he ain't had nothing but Injun whiskey over this bar in a year!''

Fatty was indignant. ''Injun whiskey, my eye!'' he exploded. ''This here's my own make, an' mighty good rye likker if I do say so! Injun whiskey!'' he snorted. ''You've been drinkin' out of horse tracks an' buffalo wallers so long you don't know a good drink when you get one!''

He placed two glasses on the bar and a bottle. Shorty poured for them both, but Fatty reached for the bottle as he put it down. ''Leave the bottle,'' I told him, ''we'll want another.'' I placed a gold piece on the bar, and Fatty picked it up so fast it looked like a wink of light.

''Better not flash that coin around if you've got more of it,'' Shorty warned. ''Especially when Wolf Kettle is around. He's the hombre you talked to out yonder, an' while Davis is away, he's ramroddin' the outfit.''

"Things look kind of slow," I suggested.

"They sure are!" Shorty's disgust was evident. "Nothing doing at all! From what we hear there's to be something big movin' soon, but you can't tell. Where you from?"

"Down Sonora way. They call me the Papago Kid."

"Shorty Carver's my handle." He looked up at me. "Sonora, is it? Well, I sure figured I knew you." He spoke softly all of a sudden. "I'd of sworn you were an hombre I saw sling a gun up to Dodge, one time. An hombre name of Wat Bell, from a Texas outfit."

"If you think I look like him," I suggested, "forget it. He might not like the resemblance!"

Shorty laughed. "Sure thing! You can be anybody you want with me. What's on your mind? You wantin' to join up?"

"Not exactly. I'm huntin' a couple of friends of mine. Bill Keys and an hombre named Taber."

Shorty Carver's face hardened. "You won't find 'em here, an' if they are friends of yours, sure you'd better hunt another sidekick than me. That Taber an' I didn't get along."

I took a sidelong look at Shorty. "He's been here then?"

"Been here?" Shorty looked around at me. "He was here yesterday!"

"What?"

My question was so sharp that a half-dozen heads turned our way, and I lowered my voice. "Did you say—*yesterday?*"

"Sure did! He rode in here about sunup, an' him an' Davis had a long confab. Then Davis takes off for Skull Valley, and where Taber went, I don't know. He rode out of here, headin' east."

For several minutes I didn't say a word. If Hugh was out here, that meant the time for a showdown had come. Yet what had I found? Nothing to date that would help. That Hugh Taylor had been known to the outlaws of Horsethief Canyon was something, but not much.

Right then I began to wonder for the first time about those absences from the ranch when Hugh was growing up. And that time he had returned with that silver-mounted saddle and a good bit of money. It was becoming more apparent where that money had come from. Had Uncle Tom Bell guessed? He was a sharp old man, and had not ridden the trails and plains for nothing. He could read sign wherever it was . . . and here was another thought: perhaps he had read the truth and guessed at what lay behind those absences and jumped Hugh about it.

Had Hugh killed his uncle?

There was enough of the old feeling for Hugh left to make me revolt at the idea, and yet it began to seem more and more possible. Uncle Tom and I had a violent quarrel and I left. What would be easier than to kill him and let me take the blame? Hugh's surprise at my sudden return could have come from his consternation at what it might mean to him, and also he might have believed those rumors that I had been killed in Mexico.

Certainly, he managed to get me out of the country without seeing anyone else.

The swinging doors shoved wide and Kettle came in. He took a sidelong glance at me and walked up to the bar at my side and ordered a drink. I could smell trouble coming and could see there was something in Kettle's craw.

He got his drink and turned to me. "We don't welcome strangers here!" he said. "State your business, an' ride on out!"

That turned me around, but I took my time. The man irritated me, and I didn't feel like side-stepping trouble. I was tired of running and ready for a showdown, and ready to back it with lead. "Kettle," I said clearly, "I didn't come in here to see you. I never heard of you. You may run a big herd where you come from, but where I ride that herd looks like mighty small gathering!''

His face darkened a little, and the yellow lights in his eyes were plainer. He half-turned before I spoke, but I gave it to him fast. ''Don't try to run any blazers on me, Kettle, because they won't stick. If you make rough talk with me, it's gun talk, and if you draw on me, I'll kill you!''

Shorty Carver had stepped wide of me and was standing there facing the room. What his play would be, I couldn't know. He was a friend of only a few minutes, yet there had been some spark of comradeship there such as one often finds with men of the same ilk and the same background. He spoke before either of us could make a move. ''He came to see Taber and Keys,'' Shorty warned, ''they sent for him!''

''What?'' Carver's statement obviously stopped Kettle. ''How do you know that?''

''Because I told him,'' I said simply.

He glared at me suspiciously. Something was gnawing at the man, and it might be something about me, but I had the feeling that he was naturally mean, a trouble hunter, a man with a burr under his saddle. ''Where'd you know Taber?'' he demanded.

''In Texas,'' I said calmly, ''and I knew

Bill Keys in Sonora." That last was sheer hope, for whether Keys had ever been below the Border, I didn't know.

"He's the Papago Kid," Carver said.

"Never heard of him!" Kettle returned sharply.

Another man spoke up, a lean-faced man with a drooping black mustache. "I have," he said. "He's the hombre that killed Albie Dick."

Kettle's eyes sharpened, and I knew that meant something to this man. Albie Dick had been a dangerous man, and a killer with fifteen dead men on his trail when we tangled in Sonora.

"That's neither here nor there," I said calmly. "I want to talk to Howie Taber!"

"You'll have to wait," Kettle said grudgingly. "He ain't here."

Somehow, the men relaxed. Shorty returned to the bar and took another drink. Under his breath, he warned, "You'd better watch yourself. Wolf was never braced like that before. He'll be careful to make his play at the right time, but you've got trouble. The man's mean as a rattler."

He downed his drink. "Also," he added, "I'm beginning to remember things. That Wat Bell who downed that man in Abilene was ramrodding an XY herd . . . and that's the ranch we're going to use in Texas!''

"What do you mean? Going to use?"

He looked at me quickly, sharply. "So? You don't know the inside on this, do you?" He was silent, tracing circles on the bar with the bottom of his glass. "Just what is between you and Taber, Kid?"

That was a sticker, and I hesitated. Shorty had said earlier that he had no use for Taber. Right then I knew my time here was short, and a friend would be a help. Another enemy would be little worse. "Taber's my cousin," I said frankly, speaking low. "I think he killed my uncle and framed me with the murder while I was in Mexico. Furthermore, I think he sent me out here to lay low and planned to have me murdered when I arrived.''

Quietly, I explained in as few words as possible and from time to time he nodded. "Glad you told me," he said. "Also there's no posters on Wat Bell out here, so you must be right on figuring that Lynch was out to get you."

"No posters on me? How do you know that?"

He grinned, and he said softly. "Because I'm a Cattle Association detective, pardner, an' I'm studyin' into the biggest steal of horses an' cattle ever organized!''

Together we walked outside, and the story
he told me answered a lot of questions. For
several years a steady stream of stolen stock
had been sent south over the old horsethief
trail from the Hole in the Wall and Robber's
Roost to Mexico, and this valley was one of the
important way stations. Lately, it had become
apparent that even larger things were in the
wind, for a man lately associated with the gang
had suddenly become owner of a Panhandle
ranch in Texas. There was a reported tie-up
with the XY in central southern Texas, and
large quantities of stock had begun to disappear
and move south toward the Border. It had begun to look as if mass stealings of stock had
begun, moving south under cover and with large
ranches as way stations.

"Who's behind it?" I asked him. "Any
guesses on that?"

"Uh huh. There is." Shorty Carver lit a
smoke. "Howie Taber's behind it. That cousin
of yours has turned out to be the brains of the
biggest stock-stealing ring in the country."

From the time he was sixteen until he was
twenty, Hugh Taylor had been absent from the
XY. He had gone again shortly after, and obviously, he had been gone at least once during the
time I was in Mexico. It was then, no doubt,
that he had begun to round up old cronies of his

251

earlier days and build the ring that Carver now told me about.

"Shorty," I said, "can you slip out of here?"

"Uh huh."

"Then wire the sheriff in Dimmit County. See if I'm really wanted there for murder. Also, check on Tom Bell's will, see who that XY spread was left to when he died. I'm having a talk with that cousin of mine!" I hesitated, thinking. "See you at the Tin Cup!"

"Watch your step!" Shorty warned. "Hugh isn't so bad, but you watch Bill Keys and Kettle!"

Chapter V
Power of the Papago Kid

After he was gone, I idled around, getting the lay of the land and thinking things over. It was well along in the afternoon, and night soon to come. By this time Hugh would know that I was still alive, that the plot to get me at the Tin Cup had failed. Evidently, the Tin Cup had been chosen because of its secluded position, and Lynch and Keys had been informed by the friend where I had stopped last that I was coming. Accordingly, they had evidently waited. It might be that I had been spotted and reported at several places since then, and they had come out to meet me, either at the Tin Cup or on the trail near there.

Probably they had managed to get Ludlow away from his ranch, or had reason to believe he would be away. Then they had either killed him by mistake, or had killed him because he returned too soon. No doubt they had plans for the Tin Cup, anyway, as the ranch was ideal for such a venture as they planned.

The jumpiness was in me now that presaged danger. I could sense it all around me, and I was restless. Every man here would be an enemy once it was realized who I was, and at any moment Bill Keys, Hugh Taylor, or Ross Lynch might ride in, and then the lid would blow off. I was surrounded by unfriendly guns, and to blast my way out would be a forlorn hope.

Mingled with the realization of my danger was an acute longing to be back with Maggie Dolliver. No woman had ever affected me as she had, and despite the fact that there was an understanding between herself and Hugh, I had the feeling that she had felt for me as I had for her. That she had brought Rowdy to me and packed the food was enough to show that she believed in me.

Time and again I walked down to the corral to talk to Rowdy. Time and again I noted exactly where my saddle was, and calculated every move it would take to resaddle him. That was something I wanted to do, but not until it was dark. To saddle him now would serve only as a warning of impending departure. I wanted them to believe that I was content to await the return of the man they knew as Howie Taber.

Yet I could feel the suspicion, and my own restlessness contributed to it. Wolf watched me sharply, his yellowish eyes rarely leaving me. Other men seemed always around, but apparently Shorty Carver had managed to slip away. Since he was accepted here, his going and coming would occasion little remark.

My thoughts kept reverting to Maggie and Win. At least Win was my friend, and it was something to have even one friend now. Once more I returned to the saloon and seated myself in a chair against the wall, careful to keep my guns clear. Evening was coming, and the sun had slipped down behind Wasson Peak and the ridges around it. All the bright glare of the Arizona sun was gone, and the desert and mountains had turned to soft pastel shades. A blue quail called out in the brush, and somewhere a burro yawned his lonely call into the cool air of twilight. A door slammed, and then I heard water splashing as someone dipped a bucket into the spring. There was a subdued murmur of voices, and the rattle of dishes. There was no hunger in me, only that poised alertness that kept my eyes moving and my every muscle and nerve aware and ready.

Casually I arose to my feet and stretched. Then, as I had a dozen times before, I sauntered carelessly down to the corral. Wolf Kettle watched me, but I ignored him, stopping near the corrals to look around. Then I stepped over and put my hand on Rowdy's neck and spoke to him. After a minute I crawled through the poles and was out of sight of Wolf or any of the others.

My movements were swift and sure. Rowdy was never bridled or saddled faster in his life, and in what seemed scarcely no time, I was sauntering back into sight, crawling once more through the corral bar. I slowly rolled a smoke, struck a match, and then ambled placidly and nonchalantly back toward the store. "Brother," I told myself, "if you get out of here with a whole skin, you're lucky."

Back in my chair I listened to the casual talk, scarcely paying attention until suddenly two horses rounded into sight. They were walking, and they came so suddenly that it was a surprise to all of us. They came from the other side of the saloon and stopped at the end of the porch opposite me.

Two men swung down. "Wolf? You got some grub ready?"

It was Hugh Taylor!

My heart pounding, I slowly lowered my hands to my knees, my eyes riveted on him.

"You'd better have!" The second man was speaking, and it was Bill Keys. "I'm hungry as a grizzly!"

It was late dusk, and no faces could be distinguished. Hugh came up on the porch, looking tall, strong, and familiar. Suddenly it was hard to think of him as being an outlaw, an enemy. I could only recall the times we went swimming together, the horses we swapped, and the times we played hooky from school and went hunting.

He happened to turn his head then, and he looked right at me. He could have seen no more than a black figure of a man, seated there, but there must have been something familiar about it. "Who's that?" His voice rang sharply.

"It's me, Hugh!" I said softly, "I figured it was about time we had a little talk."

At my voice Keys jerked like he'd been struck, and he turned. Wolf was facing me too. The three of them ringed around me, from my extreme left to full front. On the right side, the edge of the porch, there was no one.

"You . . . ? Wat?" There was an edge of something in his voice, doubt, uncertainty or something. Maybe he was remembering, too. "We've nothing to talk about, nothing at all."

"What about Uncle Tom, Hugh? I didn't kill him. . . . Did you?"

His breath drew sharply. "We won't talk about that, Wat. Not right now. You shouldn't have come here, you know that."

"Do I, Hugh? You sent me to the Tin Cup, didn't you? Was I supposed to be killed there? Did you figure to send your own cousin, who grew up with you, to get killed?"

I knew Western men. Even the outlaws were rarely cruel men. Many of them were punchers who had rustled the wrong stock once too often, some of them were men who had been too handy with a gun, but few of them were really bad men. Rather they were often reckless and careless in a land where many men were reckless and where property rights were uncertain. Among them were, of course, killers and men of criminal instincts, yet I was playing for those others.

He didn't answer me, so I went on talking, not raising my voice, just an easy conversational tone, yet all the time every nerve was on edge.

"They killed the wrong man, Hugh, and now I'm looking into things. I've been asking questions—about Uncle Tom's will, and whether I'm really wanted for murder or not, and now I'm getting mighty curious about you."

"You're too curious." His mind seemed to be made up, and I sensed an almost regretful note. "You should never have come back from Mexico, Wat. You messed up everything when you did that. You should have stayed down there. Now you're into something that's too big for you. You're playing with company that's too fast."

"Am I?" I laughed, although there was no humor in it. "No, I'm not, Hugh. You've just continued to think of me as your kid cousin. I've covered a lot of country since then, and traveled in faster company than you'll ever know."

"That's right, Boss." It was the man with the black mustache again. "This hombre is the Papago Kid. He rubbed out Albie Dick an' led the roundup of his outfit. Nobody got away."

"So the kid's grown up!" There was an edge of sarcasm in Hugh's voice. "That makes it a little better. I'd not like to be responsible for anybody taking advantage of you."

"You've still got a chance, Hugh," I said quietly. "You can break this up right now. Turn the killers of Ludlow over to the law, confess your part in this plot, and leave the country."

"Are you crazy?" He was genuinely angry now. "*You!* Giving *me* a chance!"

"Then your answer is no?" I could see that Bill Keys and Kettle were growing restive. For their taste we had talked too long, and neither of them liked the tone of it.

"You fool!" Contempt was thick in his voice. "You should never have come back from Mexico! Worse, you should have never come here! You should have hightailed it out of the country! I don't want to kill you, but there's no choice!"

There was one more thing. Nor could I resist it. "How could I leave, Hugh? I fell in love with Maggie!"

"*What?*" He wheeled so quickly to face toward me again that he gave me the one big break I'd needed. I went off that porch in one jump and ducked around the corner of the house. I'd never have dared chance it with Keys and Kettle having their eyes on me, but when Hugh turned he partially blocked them off. I hit the ground running and skidded into the shadow of a clump of mesquite. Then I gave out with a piercing whistle.

259

One shot cut the brush in reply to my whistle, but that whistle stopped them. They didn't know what it meant. It seemed like a signal and they were immediately afraid I had help nearby. It was a signal, but not for help. It was for Rowdy.

He knew what to do. On that signal he would untie himself if tied with a slip knot, or nose down corral bars. It was a trick I'd taught him, along with a dozen others.

The rattle of hooves sounded, and I heard somebody yell. "The corral's open! Somebody's there!"

I whistled again, and the big black horse wheeled between the buildings. Somebody cracked down on me again, and that time I had enough of being the target in a shooting gallery. I glimpsed a dark form and let fly, and heard a grunt, and the sound of something falling, and then I was in the saddle and taking out across the valley.

My route was in my mind. I'd gotten it from Shorty, who knew the area. Rowdy took off down Horsethief Canyon at a dead run, then slowed and turned sharply left up a trail to the bench. We had the mountain for a background and were lost in the blackness there, and Rowdy could walk like a cat when the chips were down. We crossed the shoulder of the mountain south of the ranch and hit the head of Sycamore, and down Sycamore to the trail that ran south, running parallel to Black Canyon. Then I crossed the table to the Agua Fria again, and took off up Squaw Creek.

The advantage of darkness and the best horse was mine, and I used it. Danger would come with morning, but I was hoping that Shorty would meet me at the Tumbling T with news that was good. Whatever else happened, I would see Maggie once more, and it was worth the ride and worth the danger.

———

Morning lifted the darkness away and brought back the sun-bright hills to view. I liked the feel of the country and the air on my face, and the feel of a good horse between my knees. Behind me was the end of something, the end of all the old days when I was a kid on the XY, of Uncle Tom Bell, crabby and lovable, but honest as the day—and Hugh, older than I, and skillful in all things. We'd never been close, and yet we'd done a lot together, as boys will, and we had grown older together. It is a sad thing to leave a friend behind, to find one you've admired changed.

When the sun was high I turned into a deep arroyo and found a wide shadow where I could swing down and strip the saddle from Rowdy. After I'd cared for him, I picketed him on a little grass, then slept for an hour. After I'd eaten, I saddled up again. The sun had bridged the space that divides morning from afternoon and, still blazing hot, had turned just a little toward the west when I started on. Altogether I'd spent nearly three hours in the arroyo.

The sun reflected from a distant flat rock, and the clouds left shadows on the desert floor. I studied the far reach of the valley and then kept to the low ground, moving in shadows of clouds and up washes and where the ground was broken, yet I saw no one. We were headed for a showdown, Rowdy and I, but it would be at the T, or maybe the Tin Cup. It would not be here.

———

The Tin Cup lay chill and quiet in the moonlight when Rowdy walked down the trail. We drew up, looking the place over, and it was still as death. The comparison came into my mind and made me shiver a little. That was striking too close to the truth.

Skirting the place warily, I seemed to detect a darker spot among the pines, and circled toward it. Then I drew up and listened. I heard a horse stamp and blow, then stillness.

Speaking to Rowdy so he would not whinny, I moved in.

A lone man was camped in the pines near a stream. Watching, I heard a light footfall, then turned. Shorty Carver was standing there on the edge of the brush. "Rolled my bed up an' laid out in the brush, myself," he said. "Figured it some safer. They might get wary of me."

He held out two wires, and shielding the flame with my hat, I struck a match and read them.

DISCHARGED MEXICAN HAND CONFESSED SLAYING OF BELL. NO ONE WANTED HERE.

A distinct feeling of relief hit me, just as much for Hugh as for myself. If he had taken advantage of my absence to claim the ranch all for himself, I could not have blamed him, but if he had killed Uncle Tom . . . I ripped open the other message.

TOM BELL'S WILL LEAVES XY TO WAT BELL WHEN HE RETURNS. BELL'S REASON WAS 'HE STAYED WITH ME AND HELPED TO BUILD IT.' IN EVENT OF BELL'S NOT RETURNING, RANCH TO GO TO HUGH TAYLOR.

So, then I was not a fugitive, but owner of

two hundred thousand acres of rangeland and a huge herd of cattle. Somehow, I couldn't find it in me to blame Hugh too much. Probably he had believed me killed in Mexico, and that he was the owner of the XY.

This crooked business was another thing. Uncle Tom would turn over in his grave if he thought the old XY was being used as a clearing ground or holding ground for rustled stock.

"We're heading for the T," I told Carver, "you've seen these messages?"

"Read 'em when they came in," he said. "Taylor tried to have you ambushed here. That isn't a theory anymore. We've got Ross Lynch."

"Got him? Arrested?"

"Yeah, last night. There was hell to pay in Latigo. We found Ross in the hills with some rustled stock, an' he ran for it. We got him in Latigo. He confessed on his deathbed."

Chapter VI
The Hard Way Out

Right then I knew we were in the wrong place. If Ross Lynch had been shot down and confessed, by this time Hugh would know it. So would Keys and Kettle!

In that event they would know their game

was up, and that within a matter of hours they would have posses closing down on them from all sides. Which meant that Hugh Taylor would be riding to the Tumbling T!

Or would he?

"Let's ride!" I said sharply. "He'll head for the T to see Mag, or I'm off my head! Or maybe to see me for a showdown. In any event, Keys and Kettle will want to see me, an' from what I told them at Horsethief Canyon, they'll know where to come! Let's go!"

Not waiting for Shorty to saddle, I threw a leg over Rowdy and lit out over the trail to the Tumbling T. That ride was one of the fastest I ever made on a horse, and Rowdy felt like running. We took off down the trail and skirted the cliffs until I could see the moonlight on the roofs at the T. The whole place was ablaze with lights, so I slowed down. Leaving Rowdy in the shadow of the stone stable, I moved up toward the house.

It was almost daylight, and the sky was growing gray. In the ranch yard were several horses, and I could see a dark group of them standing beyond the house, and several men were loitering about. Whoever was here was on the ground in force. On cat feet, I Injuned up to the house and slid in close to a window. Inside were several people. I could see Win Dolliver,

265

his face dark and angry, and with him was Maggie. She was as pale as he was dark, and her eyes were wide.

"He's not here and he hasn't been here in days!" Maggie was saying. "Now take your men and get out!"

"He'll come here!" That was Keys speaking. "He's gone soft on you. He told Hugh he was in love with you!"

Her eyes went to Hugh. "He said that?" Her chin lifted. "Well, all right, then! I'm in love with him!"

My heart jumped and I gripped the windowsill hard. Yet Hugh was speaking now, and I listened. "So? You sold me out, did you? You dropped me for another man?"

She turned to him. "I'm sorry, Hugh. I was intending to tell you. I was never in love with you, and you know it. I liked you, yes. You persuaded me and I listened, but I never felt sure about you, never liked the company you kept." Bill Keys laughed harshly at that. "And I hoped you'd change. You didn't.

"Then he came along, and from then on I knew there could never be anyone else."

"He beats me out of my ranch and out of my girl!" Hugh said bitterly. "That's a pretty thing!"

"I think you tried to rob him, Hugh,"

Maggie said, "and you tried to have him murdered!"

"I wish I had!" he complained bitterly.

"Boss," Keys interrupted, "let's get outside an' get the boys set. If he's comin', he'll be here soon."

"Hugh," Maggie warned, "if you don't take your men and leave here at once, I'll hate you!"

"Wouldn't that be awful!" Keys sneered.

Hugh Taylor turned on him. "Be still!" he said sharply. "I'll make the comments here!"

Keys' eyes narrowed angrily. "You'd better make 'em, then!" he snapped. "You've sure played hell with all your fancy figurin'! Mixin' this fancy doll into this has messed it up for sure! Take the boys an' light out of here! I'll take care of Mister Wat Bell when he comes!"

"You'd better get outside and wait until I come!" Hugh said sharply. "I don't want any comments made about Miss Dolliver!"

Bill Keys stared at Hugh, his eyes ugly with hatred. "Don't get high an' mighty, Taber, or whatever your name is! We follered you because you figured things right and we made money. This deal looked good until you got to mixin' women with it, but don't think we can't get shut of you just as quick if we decide we want to!"

Hugh Taylor turned on Keys. "Are you huntin' a showdown?" he demanded.

That was my cue to get away from that window. In three long, silent jumps I made it to the back door and eased inside. I took it easy, and no more than a word or two could have passed before I was just inside the kitchen and could hear them in the next room. Keys was on the prod, I could see that.

"Showdown?" Keys was saying. "I reckon there wouldn't be no showdown betwixt you an' me, Taber. If we're goin' to kill Wat Bell we'd better get outside. We can settle this later, but I'm tellin' you, don't go to givin' me orders! Not in that voice!"

Hugh's voice was icy. "All right, Keys! Let's go outside!"

I knew that tone! I'd heard it before, and this was a showdown whether Keys wanted it or not. He had ridden some rough trails since I'd known him, Hugh had, but I doubted that he was gun-slick enough to stack up right in a gun scrap with either Keys or Kettle.

Keys and Kettle went outside, and Hugh followed them. In a quick step I was into the room. Win wheeled at the sound of my movement, and Mag stood riveted where she was. "Wat! Oh, you mustn't be found here! Go away!"

"Win, you take care of her!" She had come right to my arms, and I was holding her close, looking over my shoulder at Dolliver. "Get a shotgun—you've got one, I know. Get all your shells. If the worst comes to the worst, stand them off with that. I'm going out there!"

"You're a fool to do that, Wat!" Win said seriously. "You won't have a chance, man!"

"No, I've got to side Hugh. They are going to kill him. He can't see it, either. He can't see that Keys wants a showdown. They've got the idea from him, most of the work and planning is done, so now Keys an' Kettle figure it's all over. They want to get rid of him."

"You'd side the man who tried to have you killed?" Win was incredulous.

I shrugged, knowing I was probably a fool. "He's my cousin. We grew up like brothers, and Uncle Tom would have liked it that way. Anyway, those men out there are my enemies as well as his."

From the door I took a quick, careful look at the yard. This was it, all right. Keys had walked a dozen feet away from Hugh and turned to face him. Wolf Kettle had strolled off to the right, at least fifty feet from Keys. They made two corners with Hugh Taylor as the point of the triangle.

Keys spoke first. "Taber, we don't like this

setup. We don't like you lordin' it over us an' comin' the high an' mighty around. We don't like you takin' most of the money, either. We've decided to cut you out of the deal."

Maybe I'm coldblooded, but I was curious. I wanted to see how much of the Bell blood there was in Hugh. For the first time in his life, so far as I knew, Hugh was called face to face, and if ever a man was called by a pair of curly wolves from the way back and rough, it was these two. What would he do? That was what I wondered.

For almost a half minute he didn't say anything, but he must have been thinking plenty, and when he spoke, I could have cheered. The hombre may have tried to frame me, he may have hit the wrong trails, but he was my cousin. "Why, sure, Bill!" he said. "You do want a showdown, don't you? And you, Kettle? Sure there's more of the coyote in you than the wolf. This is what they called giving a man the Black Spot in a story I read once. Funny thing, it was a pirate story, and I read it with Wat—a better man than either of you!"

He took a step further toward them, his eyes shifting from one to the other. "Spread wide, aren't you? Well, I'll take one of you to hell with me, anyway!"

Their hands were poised when I stepped out

of the door. As I stepped out, I spoke. "Which one do you want, Hugh? I'll take the other! I'm siding you!"

Keys' eyes lifted to me, then Kettle's. They weren't happy about this change in the situation, not even a little bit! Hugh did not turn a hair. "Take Kettle," he said, "Keys has been begging for it!"

"There's a good bit of skunk in both of them," I said calmly. "Trot out your coyote, Kettle! You asked for it!" I hit the ground with a jump, digging in both heels and drawing as I landed.

Kettle flashed a fast gun, I'll say that for him, and he dropped into a crouch snarling like the Wolf he was named for. I saw his gun wink red, and then I was walking into him, triggering my right-hand Colt.

Kettle fired and fired again, and then my second shot hit him just below the shirt pocket and he lifted up on his tiptoes and I slammed another one in for good measure. He went down, clawing at the dirt with both hands, and then I turned on my heel to see Hugh was down on his face, but struggling to get up, and Keys was cursing viciously and trying to get a gun up for one more shot.

"Drop it, Bill!" I yelled. "Drop it or take it!"

The face he turned on me was a mask of viciousness. Down he might be, and badly wounded, but he was a cornered cougar at that moment, boiling with all his innate viciousness. His gun came up, and I felt the shock of the bullet, then the report. I got my balance and lifted my gun, then fired. The shot turned him around on his knees and dropped him, but he wouldn't die.

With a lunge, he got to his feet. His shirt was soaked with blood and he stood there tottering and opened up on me with both guns. They turned into coughing, spitting flame, and I took another step straight forward and fired again, then shifted guns and slammed two more into him.

Still snarling, he took a step back, so full of lead he was top-heavy, but he stood there, cursing wickedly and glaring at me. Then his eyes seemed to glaze over, and mouthing curses, he went to the ground. I turned and took a look back at Kettle, but he was done for.

Looking up at the dark line of men near the horses, I told them, "This is it, boys! Drop your guns!"

They must have thought me completely crazy. I was hit once and maybe more, and my guns were almost empty, yet I was calling twelve hard-case riders, all of them gun handlers.

"That's right!" It was Shorty Carver from the barn. "Let go your belts easy! We've got you covered!"

"I'm holding a shotgun, and there's plenty of shells!" Win chimed in from the house.

They hesitated, and I didn't blame them. There were a dozen of them, but they could see the rifle from the barn, and the shotgun from the house. The rifle was a Spencer, firing a .56 caliber bullet of 360 grains. It took no great imagination to realize that while some of them might, and probably would, get away, the Spencer would account for several, and a man hit with a .56 caliber bullet doesn't travel far. As for the shotgun, it had twin barrels, and that meant two dead men without reloading. As for me, I was tottering on my feet, but I'd missed only one shot of all I'd fired, and nobody wanted to gamble I'd miss more. It was a cinch anywhere from four to seven of them would hit dirt before the rest got away. And nobody was sure he wouldn't be one of the seven.

"To hell with it!" The black-mustached man who had recalled me from Sonora let go his belts, and it was a signal. They all did likewise.

At that moment a half-dozen riders swept down the hill and into the yard. Two of them wore badges. I turned and walked slowly toward Hugh as Win and Maggie rushed from the house toward me.

Dropping on one knee, I turned Hugh over gently. His eyes flickered open, and he looked at me. There was nothing anybody could do for him. Bill Keys hadn't been missing any shots, and the only wonder was that Hugh was still alive.

"Thanks, kid!" he whispered. "You were right on time! You an' Mag . . . I'm glad! Real glad!" His breath sobbed in his lungs for three deep, agonized gasps, and then he spoke again. "Unc . . . le Tom . . . he told me why . . . left ranch . . . you. Knew I was . . . crook. . . . I was a fool."

We got him inside then, and along about three that morning, he hung up his spurs.

In another room, I was having my own trouble, for I'd taken two slugs instead of one, and the Doc had to dig one of them out. It came hard, but I had a bullet to bite on while he probed for it. Mag was with me, with me all the time, although twice I sent her to see how Hugh was coming.

He came out of it, Hugh did, just before the end, and when he did, I got out of bed and went in. Doc told me I was crazy, but I went.

He looked up at me from the bed. "It's all square, Hugh," I said. "Tell Uncle Tom hello."

"You think I'll see him?" he asked me, and his voice was mighty hoarse.

"Sure you will!" I said. "Any cowhand might take a wrong trail once, or put the wrong brand on a cow! I think the Inspector up there can read your brand right!"

"Thanks, kid," he said. "When you grew up, you sure grew tall!"

I took his hand then, and he was looking up at me when his eyes blinked and his grip tightened, then loosened. "He's all yours, boy," I said softly. "Let him have his head!"

You know, I'll swear he smiled. . . . It was really something, after all, to have a friend like Hugh.

The
Sixth Shotgun

Author's Note

A lot of people in the early days of the West did not believe in courts. They preferred to judge a culprit and execute the sentence right on the spot.

For many, it was a simple matter of expediency. Suppose you caught a man branding one of your cattle out in the field. Putting a gun on him, you took him into town, which may have been fifty miles away, to turn him over to the sheriff. You then rode back to your ranch.

In a few days you had to ride all the way back into town to testify against him, and then ride back home. Sometimes you rode four or five hundred miles just to get that one criminal taken care of.

It was thought much easier to hang the man when and where he was caught, and that was often done. It saved your horse and saved your time.

They were hanging Leo Carver on Tuesday afternoon, and the loafers were watching the gallows go up. This was the first official hanging in the history of Canyon Gap, and the first gallows ever built in the Territory. But then, the citizens at the Gap were always the kind to go in for style.

The boys from the ranches were coming in, and the hard-booted men from the mines, and the nine saloons were closing up, but only for the hour of the hanging. On the street behind the Palace where the cottonwoods lined the creek, Fat Marie had given three hours off to the girls. One for the hanging and one for mourning and the third for drinking their tears away.

For Leo had been a spending man who would be missed along the street, and Leo had been a singing man with a voice as clear as a mountain echo and fresh as a long wind through the sage. And Leo was a handsome man, with a gun too quick to his hand. So they were hanging Leo Carver on the gallows in Canyon Gap, and the folks were coming in from the forks of every creek.

From behind the barred window Leo watched them working. "Build it high!" he yelled at them. "And build it strong, for you're hanging the best man in Canyon Gap when tomorrow comes!"

Old Pap, who had prospected in the Broken Hills before the first foundation was laid at the Gap, took his pipe from his mouth and spat into the dust. "He's right, at that," he said, "and no lie. If the 'Paches were coming over that hill right now, it's Leo Carver I'd rather have beside me than any man jack in this town."

Editor Chafee nodded his head. "Nobody will deny that he's a fighting man," he agreed. "Leo was all right until civilization caught up with him."

And there it was said, a fit epitaph for him, if epitaph he'd have, and in their hearts not a man who heard it but agreed that what Chafee said was right.

"There'll be some," Old Pap added, "who'll feel a sigh of relief when they spring that trap. When Leo's neck is stretched and the sawbones says the dead word over him, many a man will stop sweating, you can bet on that."

"Better be careful what you say." Jase Ford shifted uneasily. "It ain't healthy to be hintin'."

"Not since they put Leo away, it ain't," Old Pap agreed, "but truth's a luxury the old can afford. There's nothing they can take from me but my life, and that's no use to me. And to do that they'd have to shoot me down from behind, and that's the sort of thing they'd do unless they could hang me legal, like Leo Carver's to be hung."

Nobody said anything, but Chafee looked gloomy as he stared at the gallows. There was no living doubt that Leo Carver was an outlaw. No doubt that he had rustled a few head here and there, no doubt that he had offended the nice people of the town by carousing at the Palace and down the street of the cottonwoods. There was no doubt, either, that he'd stuck up the stage that night on the Rousensock—but from there on there was doubt a-plenty.

Mitch Williams was dead, buried out there on boot hill with the others gone before him— Mitch Williams, the shotgun messenger who never lost a payload until that night on Rousensock, the night that Leo Carver stuck up the stage.

———

It was a strange story no matter how you looked at it, but Leo was a strange man, a strange man of dark moods and happy ones, but a man with a queer streak of gallantry in him and something of a manner all his own.

Mitch had been up on the box that night when Leo Carver stepped from the brush. Oh, he was wearing a mask, all right, wearing a mask that covered his face. But who did not know it was Leo?

He stepped from the brush with a brace of six-guns in his hands and said, "Hold those horses, Pete! You can—" He broke off sharp there, for he saw Mitch.

Now Mitch Williams was a hand. He had that shotgun over his knees but the muzzle was away from Leo. Mitch could never have swung that shotgun around under Leo's gun, and he knew it. So did Doc Spender, who was stage driver. Leo Carver had that stage dead to rights and he had Mitch Williams helpless.

"Sorry, Mitch!" He said it loud and clear, so they all heard him. "I thought this was your night off. I'd never rob a stage you were on, and I'd never shoot you or force you to shoot me." He swung his horse. "So long!" And he was gone.

That was Leo for you. That was why they liked him along the Gila, and why as far away as the Nueces they told stories about him. But what happened after that was different.

The stage went on south. It went over the range through Six-Shooter Gap and there was another holdup. There was a sudden blast of fire from the rocks and Mitch Williams toppled dead from the box, and then another blast—it was a shotgun—and Doc took a header into the brush and coughed out his life there in the mesquite.

Inside they were sitting still and frightened. They heard somebody crawl up to the box and throw it down. They heard it hit, and then they heard somebody riding off. One horse, one rider.

The next morning they arrested Leo.

He was washing up at the time, and they'd waited for just that. He had his guns off and they took him without a fight. Not that he tried to make one. He didn't. He just looked surprised.

"Aw, fellers," he protested. "I never done nothing! What's the matter?"

"You call that nothing? You robbed the stage last night."

"Oh, that?" He just grinned. "Put down those guns, boys. I'll come along. Sure, you know by this time I didn't rob it. I just stuck it up for a lark, and when I seen Mitch, I knowed it was no lark. That hombre would have sat still while I robbed it and drilled me when I left. He was a trusty man, that one."

"You said 'was,' so I guess you know you killed him."

285

Leo's face changed then. "Killed who? Say, what is this?"

And then they told him, and his face turned gray and sick. He looked around at their faces and none of them were friendly. Mitch had been a family man, and so had Doc. Both of them well liked.

"I didn't do it," Leo said. "That was somebody else. I left 'em be."

"Until you could get a shotgun!" That was Mort Lewand, who shipped the money for the bank. "Like you said, Mitch would shoot. You knew that, and he had the gun on you, so you backed out. Then you came back later with a shotgun and shot him from ambush."

"That's not true." Leo was dead serious. "And he didn't have me covered. Mitch had that shotgun pointed the other way. I had the drop and if I'd been planning to kill him, I'd've shot him then."

———

Oh, they had a trial! Judge come over from Tucson to hold court. They had a trial and a big one. Folks come from all over, and they made a big thing of it. Not that there was much anybody could say for Leo.

Funny thing, that is. Most of us, right down inside, we knowed the kind of man Leo Carver was, but most of what we knew wasn't evidence. Ever stop to think how hard it is to know a man isn't a murderer and yet know that your feeling he isn't ain't evidence?

They made it sound bad. Leo admitted he had killed seven men. Fair, stand-up fights, but still the men were dead by his gun. He admitted to rustling a few cows. Leo could have denied it, and maybe they couldn't have proved it in a court of law, but Leo wasn't used to the ways of courts and he knowed darn well we all knew he had rustled them cows. Fact is, I don't think he ever thought of denying it.

He had stuck up a few stages, too. He even admitted to that. But he denied killing Mitch Williams and he denied getting that box.

Twenty thousand, it held. Twenty thousand in gold.

Everybody thought Webb Pascal would defend Leo, but he refused, said he wanted no part of it. Webb had played poker with Leo and they'd been friends, but Webb refused him. Leo took that mighty hard. Lane Moore refused him, too, so all he could do was get that drunken old Bob Keyes to handle his case.

Convicted? You know he was. That's why they are hanging him. Keyes couldn't defend a sick cat from a bath. When they got through asking questions of Leo Carver, he was a dead Injun, believe me.

He had tried to stick up the stage once. He was a known killer. He had rustled cows. He traveled with a bad element in Canyon Gap. He had no alibi. All he had, really, was his own statement that he hadn't done it—that and the thing we knew in our hearts that isn't admissible as evidence.

"Shame for you fellers to go to all that trouble," Leo said now. That was Leo. There's no stopping him. "Why don't we just call the whole thing off?"

Mort Lewand stood in his doorway chewing his cigar and watching that gallows go up, and it made me sore, seeing it like that, for if ever one man had hated another, Mort Lewand had hated Leo.

Why? No particular reason. Personality, I'd guess you'd say. It was simply that they never tied up right. Mort, he pinched every dime he made. Leo spent his or gave it away. Mort went to church regular and was a rising young businessman. He was the town's banker and he owned the express company, and he had just bought one of the finest ranches in the country.

Leo never kept any money. He was a cattleman when he wanted to be, and as steady a hand as you'd find when he worked. One time he saved the CY herd almost singlehanded when they got caught in a norther. He took on the job of ramrodding the Widow Ferguson's ranch after her old man was killed, and he tinkered and slaved and worked, doing the job of a half-dozen hands until she had something she could see for money enough to keep her.

Leo never kept a dime. He ate it up, drank it up, gave it away. The rest of the time he sat under the cottonwoods and played that old guitar of his and sang songs, old songs like my mother used to sing, old Scotch, Irish, and English songs, and some he made up as he went along.

He got into fights too. He whipped the three Taylor boys singlehanded one day. I remember that most particular because I was there. That was the day he got the blood on Ruth Hadlin's handkerchief.

———

The Hadlins were the town's society. Every town's got some society, and Judge Emory Hadlin was the big man of this town. He had money, all right, but he had name too. Even in the West some folks set store by a name, and whenever the judge said his name it was like ringing a big gong. It had a sound. Maybe that was all some names had, but this one had more.

Honor, reputation, square dealing, and no breath of scandal ever to touch any of them.

Fine folks, and everybody knew it. Mort Lewand, he set his cap for Ruth but she never seemed to see him. That made him some angered, but tickled most of us. Mort figured he was mighty high-toned and it pleased us when Ruth turned him down flat.

Don't get the idea she was uppity. There was that time Old Pap come down with pneumonia. He was in a bad way and nobody to look after him but little Mary Ryan from down on the Street. Mary cared for him night and day almost until Ruth Hadlin heard about it.

She came down there and knocked on the door, and when Mary opened it and saw Ruth she turned seven colors. There she was, a mighty pert little girl, but she was from the Street, and here was Ruth Hadlin—well, they don't come any further apart.

Mary flushed and stammered and she didn't know what to say, but Ruth came right on in. She turned around and said, "How is he, Mary? I didn't even know he was ill."

Ill, that's what she said. We folks mostly said sick instead of ill. Mary was shocked, too, never guessing that anybody like Ruth would know her name, or speak to her like that.

"He's bad off, Miss Ruth, but you shouldn't be here. This is the—it's the Street."

Ruth just looked at her and smiled, and she

said, "I know it is, Mary, but Old Pap is ill and he can be just as ill on the Street as anywhere. I just heard about it, Mary, and how you've been caring for him. Now you go get some rest. I'll stay with him."

Mary hesitated, looking at that beautiful blue gown Ruth was wearing and at the shabby little cabin. "There ain't—isn't much to do," she protested.

"I know." Ruth was already bending over Old Pap and she just looked around and said, "By the way, Mary, tell somebody to go tell Doctor Luther to come down here."

"We tried, miss. He won't come. He said all his business was the other side of town, that he'd no time for down here."

Ruth straightened up then. "You go tell him that Ruth Hadlin wants him down here!" Her voice was crisp. "He'll come."

He did, too.

But that was Miss Ruth. She was a thoroughbred, that one. And that was where she first met Leo Carver.

It was the third day she had been sharing the nursing with Mary Ryan, and she was in the shack alone when she heard that horse. He was coming hell bent for election and she heard him pull up in front of the house and then the door opened and in stepped Leo Carver.

She knew him right off. How could you miss him? He was two inches over six feet, with shoulders wider than two of most men, and he was dark and clean-built with a fine line to his jaw and he had cold gray eyes. He wore two guns and his range clothes, and right then he had a two-day growth of beard. It must have startled her. Here was a man known as an outlaw, a rustler, and a killer, and she was there alone with a sick man.

He burst in that door and then drew up short, looking from Ruth to the sick old man. If he was surprised to find her there, he didn't let on. He just swept off his hat and asked, "How is he, Miss Hadlin?"

For some reason she was excited. Frightened, maybe. "He's better," she said. "Miss Ryan and I have been nursing him."

Mary had come into the room behind him, and now she stepped around quickly. "He's a lot better, Leo," she said.

"Maybe I can help nurse him, then," Carver said. He was looking at Ruth and she was white-faced and large-eyed.

Old Pap opened one eye. "Like hell," he said expressively. "You think I want a relapse? You get on out of here. Seems like," he protested plaintively, "every time I git to talk to a good-lookin' gal, somebody comes hornin' in!"

Leo grinned then and looked from Ruth to Mary. "He's in his right mind, anyway," he said, and left.

Mary stood there looking at Ruth, and Ruth looked after Leo and then at Mary.

"He's—he's an outlaw," Ruth said.

Mary Ryan turned very sharp toward Ruth, and I reckon it was the only time she ever spoke up to Ruth. "He's the finest man I ever knew!"

And the two of them just stood there looking at each other and then they went to fussing over Old Pap. That was the longest convalescence on record.

But there was that matter of the blood on her handkerchief. Ruth Hadlin was coming down the street and she was wearing a beautiful gray dress and a hat with a veil—very uptown and big city.

She was coming down the boardwalk and everybody was turning to look—she was a fine figure of a woman and she carried herself well— and just then the doors of the Palace burst open and out comes a brawling mass of men swinging with all their fists. They spilled past Ruth Hadlin into the street and it turns out to be the three Taylors and Leo Carver.

They hit dirt and came up swinging. Leo smashed a big fist into the face of Scott Taylor and he went over into the street. Bob rushed him and Leo ducked and took him around the knees, dumping him so hard the ground shook.

Bully Taylor was the tough one, and he and Leo stood there a full half-minute slugging it out with both hands, and then Leo stepped inside and whipped one to Bully's chin and the pride of the Taylors hit dirt, out so cold he's probably sleeping yet.

Ruth Hadlin had stopped in her tracks, and now Leo stepped back and wiped the blood from his face with a jerk and some of it spattered on Ruth's handkerchief. She cried out. He turned around and then he turned colors.

"Miss Hadlin," he said with a grin on his face, "I'm right sorry. I'd no intention getting blood on you, but"—and he grinned—"it's good red blood, even if it isn't blue."

She looked at him without turning a hair, and then she said coolly, "Don't stand there with your face all bloody. Go wash it." And then she added just as coolly, "And next time don't lead with your right. If he hadn't been so all in, he'd have knocked you out." With that she walks off up the street and we all stood there staring.

Leo, he stared most of all. "Well, I'm a skinned skunk!" he said. "Where do you reckon she ever heard about leading with a right?"

Mary Ryan, she heard about it, but she said

nothing, just nothing at all, and that wasn't Mary's way. Of course, we all knew about Mary. She was plumb crazy about Leo but he paid no particular attention to any one of the girls. Or all of them, for that matter.

There was talk around town, but there always is. Some folks said this was as good a time as any to get shut of Leo Carver and his like. That it was time Canyon Gap changed its ways and spruced up a bit. Mort Lewand was always for changing things. He even wanted to change the name of Canyon Gap to Hadlin. It was the judge himself who stopped that.

———

So we sat around now and listened to the hammers and thought of how big an occasion it was to be. Some of the folks from the creek were already in town, camped out ready for the big doings tomorrow.

Ruth Hadlin was not around and none of us gave it much thought. All of this was so far away from the Hadlin folks. Ruth bought a horse, I remember, about that time. It was a fine big black. The Breed done sold it to her.

Funny thing, come to think of it, because I'd heard him turn down five hundred for that horse—and that in a country where you get a good horse for twenty dollars—but Ruth had ways and nobody refused her very much. What she wanted with a horse that big I never could see.

Editor Chafee, he hoisted his britches and was starting back toward the shop when Ruth Hadlin came down the street. She stopped nearby and she looked at that gallows. Maybe her face was a little pale, but the fact that all those rough-necks were around never seemed to bother her.

"Tom," she said right off, "what do you believe Leo Carver did with that money?" Chafee rubbed his jaw. "You know," he scowled, "I've studied about that. I can't rightly say."

"What has he always done with it before?"

"Why, he spent it. Just as fast as he could."

"I wonder why he didn't use it to hire a better lawyer? He could have had a man from El Paso for that. Or for much less! A good lawyer might have freed him."

"I wondered about that." Chafee looked a little anxiously at Mort Lewand. Mort was a power in town and he disliked Carver and made no secret of it. Lewand was looking that way, and now he started over. "It doesn't really matter now, does it?" Chafee added.

Lewand came up and looked from one to the other. Then he smiled at Ruth. "Rather noisy, isn't it, Ruth? Would you like me to escort you home?"

"Why, thank you," she said sweetly, "but

I think I'll stay. I've never seen a gallows before. Have you, Mr. Lewand?''

"Me?" He looked startled. "Oh, yes. In several places."

She stood there a few minutes watching the carpenters work. ''Well,'' Ruth said slowly, ''it's too bad, but I'm glad no local people lost anything in that holdup.''

We all looked at her, but she was watching the gallows, an innocent smile on her lips.

Editor Chafee cleared his throat. ''I guess you weren't told, Miss Hadlin. The fact is, that money belonged to Mort here.''

She smiled brightly. Women are strange folk. ''Oh, no, Tom. You've been misinformed! As a matter of fact, that money was a payment on Mr. Lewand's ranch, and when he consigned it for carriage it became the property of the former owner of the ranch. That was the agreement, wasn't it, Mr. Lewand?''

For some reason it made Mort mad, but he nodded. ''That's right.''

Ruth nodded too. ''Yes, Mr. Lewand was telling me about it. He's very farsighted, I think. Isn't that wonderful, Tom? Just think how awful it would have been if he had paid that whole twenty thousand dollars and then lost it and had to pay it over! My, it would take a wealthy man to do that, wouldn't it now?''

297

Editor Chafee was looking thoughtful all of a sudden, and Old Pap had taken the pipe from his lips and was staring at Ruth. Mort, he looked mad as a horny toad, though for the life of me, I couldn't see why. After all, it had been a smart stunt.

"Those awful shotguns!" From the way she was talking you wouldn't have believed that girl had a brain in her head. "I don't believe people should be allowed to own them. I wonder where Leo got the one he used?"

"Claimed he never owned one," Chafee commented slowly.

"He probably borrowed one from a friend," Mort said carelessly. "I suppose they are easy to find."

"That's just it!" Ruth exclaimed. "The man who loaned him that shotgun is just as guilty as he is. I think something should be done about it."

"I doubt if anybody loaned him one," Mort said, offhand. "He probably stole it."

"Oh, no! Because," she added hastily, "if he did, he returned it. Everybody in town who owns a shotgun still has it. There are only six of them in Canyon Gap. Daddy has two, Editor Chafee has one, Pap here has an old broken one, and Mitch always carried one."

"That's only five," Old Pap said softly.

"Oh!" Ruth put her fingers to her mouth.

298

"How silly of me. I'd forgotten yours, Mr. Lewand."

There was the stillest silence I ever did hear, with nobody looking at anybody else. Suddenly Ruth looked at a little watch she had, gasped something about being late, and started off.

Editor Chafee began to fill his pipe, and Old Pap scratched his knee, and all of us just sat there looking a lot dumber than we were. Mort Lewand didn't seem to know what to say, and what he finally said didn't help much. "If a man wanted to find a shotgun," he said, "I don't suppose he'd have much trouble." With that he turned and walked off.

You know something? The sound of those hammers wasn't a good sound. Editor Tom Chafee scratched his chin with the stem of his pipe. "Pete," he says to me, "you were supposed to ride shotgun that night. Whose shotgun would you have used?"

"Mitch always lent me his. I was feeling poorly and Mitch took over for me. Leo, he called my name when he first rode up, if you recall."

That shotgun business was bothering all of us. Where *did* Leo get a shotgun? This was rifle and pistol country, and shotguns just weren't plentiful. Ruth Hadlin could have narrowed it down even more, because everybody knew that Judge Hadlin wouldn't let anybody touch one of his guns but himself. They were expensive, engraved guns, and he kept them locked up in a case.

Where had Leo picked up a shotgun? What had he done with the money?

Editor Chafee looked down at Old Pap all of a sudden. "Pap," he said, "let's walk over to my place. You, too, Pete. I want you to look at my shotgun."

We looked at that gun and she was all covered with grease and dust. That shotgun hadn't been fired in six months, anyway. Or for a long time. It certainly hadn't been the gun that killed Mitch and Doc.

"Just for luck," Chafee said seriously, "we'd better go have a look at the judge's guns."

Behind us we could hear those hammers a-pounding, and we could hear O'Brien rehearsing his German band. From where we walked we could see six or seven wagons coming down the road, all headed into Canyon Gap, for the hanging.

———

Certain things happened that I didn't hear until later. I didn't hear about Ruth Hadlin, all pretty as ever a picture could be, walking into that jail to see Leo Carver. When she got into the office the sheriff was standing there looking down at a cake on his desk. That cake had been cut and it was some broken up because he had taken two files from it. Mary Ryan was standing by his side.

Sheriff Jones looked mighty serious. "Mary," he was saying, "this here's a criminal offense, helping a man to break jail. Now, where's those other two files? No use you stalling—I know you bought four of 'em."

"You're so smart," she said, "you find 'em!" She tossed her head at him and gave him a flash of those saucy eyes of hers.

Sheriff Jones leaned over the table. "Now look, Mary," he protested, "I don't want to make trouble for you, but we just can't have no prison break. Why, think of all those folks coming for miles to see a hanging! They'd be mad enough to string *me* up."

"Why not?" she said, short-like. "He's no more guilty than you are."

Jones started to protest again and then he looked up and saw Ruth Hadlin standing there in the door. Her face was cool as she could make it, and, mister, that was cold! In one hand she held Leo's guitar.

The sheriff straightened up, mighty flustered. Here he was, talking confidential-like

301

with a girl from the Street! Suppose that got around among the good folks of the town. Be as much as his job was worth, and election coming up too.

He flushed and stammered. "This here—this young woman," he spluttered, "she was trying to smuggle files to the prisoner. She—"

Ruth Hadlin interrupted, her eyes cold and queenlike on the sheriff. "I can assure you, Sheriff Jones, that I am not at all interested in your relations with this young lady, nor in the subject of your conversation.

"I have brought this guitar to the prisoner," she continued. "I understand he enjoys singing, and we think it cruel and inhuman that he be forced to listen to that banging and hammering while they build a gallows on which to hang him. It is cruel torture."

Jones was embarrassed. "He don't mind, ma'am," he protested. "Leo, he's—"

"May I take this instrument to him, Sheriff Jones?" Her voice was cold. "Or do you want to examine me? Do you think I might be smuggling files too?"

Sheriff Jones was embarrassed. The very idea of laying a hand on Ruth Hadlin, the daughter of old Judge Emory Hadlin, gave him cold shivers.

"No, no, ma'am! Of course not." He gestured toward the cells. "Just you give it to him, ma'am! I'm sorry. I—"

"Thank you, Sheriff." Ruth swept by him and up to the cell.

"Young man,"—her voice was clear—"I understand that you play a guitar, so I have brought you this one. I hope the music that you get out of it will make your heart free."

Leo looked startled, and he took the guitar through the bars. "Thank you, Miss Hadlin," he said politely. "I wish—" He broke off, his face a little flushed. "I wish you didn't have to see me in here. You see, I didn't—I never killed those men. I'd like you to believe that."

"What I believe," Ruth said sweetly, "is of no importance. The music from the guitar will be pleasant for you, if played in private." She turned abruptly and walked out, and she went by Sheriff Jones like a pay-car past a tramp.

Mary told it afterwards, and Mary said that Leo plunked a string on that guitar and then he looked at it, funny-like. "It sure didn't sound right," Mary said. I shouldn't wonder.

That was late Monday afternoon. By sundown there was maybe two hundred people camped around town waiting for the big hanging next afternoon. Old Pap, he wasn't around, nor was Editor Chafee. Some said that when they left the judge's house, the judge himself was riding with them.

When next I come across Old Pap, he was standing on the corner looking at that gallows. That was near the jail, and from the window Leo could see us.

"Folks would be mighty upset if they missed their hanging, Pap," Leo said.

"They won't!" Pap was mighty short and gruff. "They'll git their hanging, and don't you forget it."

That gallows looked mighty ghostly standing there in the twilight, and it didn't make me feel no better. Leo, well, he always seemed a right nice feller. Of course, he had rustled a few head, but I wouldn't want to take no oath I hadn't, nor Old Pap, nor most of us. Leo, he was just a young hellion, that was all.

Even when he stuck up those stages he just done it for drinking money. Not that I'm saying it's right, because I know it ain't, but them days and times, folks excused a lot of a young man who was full of ginger, long as he didn't hurt nobody and was man enough.

Especially of Leo's sort. If you was in trouble you just let him know. Come prairie fire, flood, stampede, or whatever, Leo was your man. No hour was too late, no job too miserable for him to lend a hand. And never take a dime for it.

So we all went to bed, and the last thing Leo said was, "I never did cotton to no rope necktie. I don't figure it's becoming."

"Wait'll tomorry," Old Pap said.

———

The sun was no more than up before the lid blew off the town. Somebody yelled and folks came a-running. I slid into my pants and scrambled outside. The crowd was streaming toward the Plaza and I run down there with 'em. The bars was out of the jail window, filed off clean as you'd wish, then bent back out of the way. Tied to one of them was a sheet of paper. It was a note:

"Sorry I couldn't wait, but I don't think you folks want me hanging around here, anyway."

Mary Ryan was there by the jail. She had tears in her eyes but she looked pleased as a polecat in a henhouse too. Sheriff Jones, he took on something fierce.

"Figured she was talking poetry," he said angrily. "She told him the music he'd get out of that guitar would make his heart free. No wonder Mary wouldn't tell me what became of the other two files."

One big bearded man with hard eyes stared at the sheriff with a speculative eye. "What about the hanging?" he demanded. "We drove fifty mile to see a hanging."

Editor Tom Chafee, Judge Emory Hadlin, and Old Pap came up around them. They looked across the little circle at Jones.

"Ruth figured it right," the judge said. "Only six shotguns in town. My two shotguns, and by the dust of the cases you can see they'd not been disturbed; Editor Chafee's, which hadn't been cleaned in months; Old Pap's was broke, and Mitch had his with him. That leaves just one more shotgun."

Everybody just stood there, taking it all in and doing some figuring. Suppose that twenty thousand never left the bank? Or suppose it did leave and it was recovered by the man sending it? His debt would be paid and he would still have the money, and a young scamp like Leo Carver'd be blamed for it all.

Of course, Leo was gone. Some folks said he rode that big black Ruth Hadlin bought. What happened to that horse we never did know, because Ruth was gone, too, and her gray mare.

The trail headed west, the trail they left, and somebody living on the edge of town swore he heard two voices singing something about being bound for Californy.

We figured the judge would about burst a gasket, but he was a most surprising man. Something was said about it by somebody and all he did was smile a little.

"Many's a thoroughbred," he said, "was a frisky colt. Once they get the bridle on 'em, they straighten out. As far as that goes," he added, "every blue-blooded family can use a little red blood!"

So everybody was happy. We celebrated mighty big. I reckon the biggest in the history of Canyon Gap. O'Brien's German band played, and everybody had plenty to eat and drink.

The folks that came for the hanging wasn't disappointed, either. They got what they wanted. They got their hanging, all right. Maybe it wasn't a legal hanging, but it was sure satisfactory.

We hung Mort Lewand.

About Louis L'Amour

*"I think of myself in the oral tradition—
as a troubadour, a village taleteller,
the man in the shadows of the camp-
fire. That's the way I'd like to be
remembered—as a storyteller. A good
storyteller."*

It is doubtful that any author could be as at
home in the world recreated in his novels as
Louis Dearborn L'Amour. Not only could he
physically fill the boots of the rugged characters he
wrote about, but he literally "walked the land my
characters walk." His personal experiences as well
as his lifelong devotion to historical research com-
bined to give Mr. L'Amour the unique knowledge
and understanding of people, events, and the
challenge of the American frontier that became
the hallmarks of his popularity.

Of French-Irish descent, Mr. L'Amour could
trace his own family in North America back to
the early 1600s and follow their steady progres-
sion westward, "always on the frontier." As a
boy growing up in Jamestown, North Dakota,
he absorbed all he could about his family's
frontier heritage, including the story of his great-
grandfather who was scalped by Sioux warriors.

Spurred by an eager curiosity and desire to broaden his horizons, Mr. L'Amour left home at the age of fifteen and enjoyed a wide variety of jobs including seaman, lumberjack, elephant handler, skinner of dead cattle, assessment miner, and officer on tank destroyers during World War II. During his "yondering" days he also circled the world on a freighter, sailed a dhow on the Red Sea, was shipwrecked in the West Indies and stranded in the Mojave Desert. He won fifty-one of fifty-nine fights as a professional boxer and worked as a journalist and lecturer. He was a voracious reader and collector of rare books. Mr. L'Amour's personal library of some 10,000 volumes covers a broad range of scholarly disciplines including many personal papers, maps, and diaries of the pioneers.

Mr. L'Amour "wanted to write almost from the time I could talk." After developing a widespread following for his many adventure stories written for fiction magazines, Mr. L'Amour published his first full-length novel, *Hondo*, in the United States in 1953. Every one of his more than 100 books is in print; there are nearly 230 million copies of his books in print worldwide, making him one of the bestselling authors in modern literary history. His books have been translated into twenty languages, and more than forty-five of his novels and stories have been made into feature films and television movies.

His hardcover bestsellers include *The Lonesome Gods*, *The Walking Drum* (his twelfth-century historical novel), *Jubal Sackett*, *Last of the Breed*, and *The Haunted Mesa*. His memoir, *Education of a Wandering Man*, was a leading hardcover nonfiction bestseller in 1989.

Audio dramatizations and adaptations of many L'Amour stories are available on cassette tapes from Bantam Audio Publishing.

The recipient of many great honors and awards, in 1983 Mr. L'Amour became the first novelist ever to be awarded the National Gold Medal by the United States Congress in honor of his life's work. In 1984 he was also awarded the Medal of Freedom by President Reagan.

Louis L'Amour died on June 10, 1988. His wife, Kathy, and their two children, Beau and Angelique, carry the L'Amour tradition forward.